A STORY ON THE AMERICAN DREAM

MATTHEW BOBBITT

ON PIEDMONT'S PLOT

LEVIATHAN IMPRINT

WALLA WALLA

ON PIEDMONT'S PLOT. First Print Edition.
Copyright © 2019, 2025 by Matthew Bobbitt.

ISBN 979-8-9935049-0-2

For more information, contact:

Leviathan Imprint
14 East Main Street, Suite 216
Walla Walla, Washington
99362

For Don.

Table of Contents

On The Long Train Ride
5

The Pleasant Pheasant
12

The Sheriff Brainerd Dice
26

Back To Work
46

This Grand Ol' American Dream
53

The Story of Ol' Iron
57

The Identification of Constance Lowrey
67

Thing To Understand 'bout The Bountyman
71

Nancy & Narcissa
75

"That Seem A Bit Odd Ta You?"
81

Moonlight Down The Valley
85

The Dead Part
87

A Cat, And A Big One, And A Male
89

Lightnin' In A Bottle
96

The Confrontation With Constance Lowrey
99

The Property, Not Its Owner
133

Melvina's
139

The Old Kirkman Place, On Colville
142

First Piano Concer·to, Second Movement
144

ON THE LONG
TRAIN RIDE

✝

Patience, I remind the reader, is a virtue. It is thus I would forewarn that, though this may be hardly the way to begin such an account, our protagonist does not mark his first appearance until the next chapter. In fact, for reasons which will be made apparent soon enough, this chapter does not concern the primary action up on Piedmont's Plot atall. So should the more impatient—or the more anxious—among readers wish to pass this chapter by, such may be a perfectly sufficient way to enjoy this story; perhaps leaving this opening chapter for last, to be returned to after experiencing the tale in full, and so having gained fuller insight into the revelations behind these preliminary words. In my view, however, the story of the Piedmont Plot is best experienced through glass of a certain prefatory hue; hence this prefatory chapter. Not a preface quite, but nonetheless something thereof:

To begin, then, in earnest, I would offer an observation: Though it is generally but once, or at best twice, a man should expect to confront the prospect of his own demise, even in that normal case, where a man has his long life entire to venerate death, his final moments will near-surely give that he did not make the most of what was provided; or he'll look back on his years and lament that he was not given a fair shake, or even when well-advanced in his years he will oft feel he was not provided time sufficient to do all that could have been done.

This is only moreso in the untimely case, or the unexpected one—a man finding himself on the wrong end of the gun, face-to some untamed predator, perhaps his neck in the noose, or even just too-high up an unstable ladder. But again regardless, even this unlooked-for exam will offer the same result; only undertaken, yes more hastily, but shall we also say more harshly.

Though I cannot speak from direct experience, the tales I've heard from the survivors of-such suggest that in either case the resulting effect is hardly one of consolation. Rather it will be quite the opposite; in general the mood of one's closing moments will be sadness, loss or, most-oft, regret.

And then, typically, that's the end of it. Fate either has its way or, as in the case of my examples, the fellow is lucky enough to see another day; and will, in some probability, make attempt, for some time at least, to make something better of himself; though sometimes he will not.

In pondering this, over my years, though, I have come to wonder if it must follow that such ultimate confrontations should also befall the rare man who *is* at an adequate station in his life and who, in such circumstance, finds that he did *not* squander his life and *was* given of things fairly and in fact *is* satisfied with what he's done with what was provided; and so in his final moments lacks cause to feel such sadness, nor loss, nor that dread regret.

Which begs what such a man *does* feel.

It is rare indeed but I have twice had occasion to come-across such a fellow, and I was careful, on both occasions, to examine the man close the moment I caught on and to collect what I could of an impression; on how it was he thought to conduct himself, how he presented his visage, and even with which words he chose his tone:

On the first occasion the man was what you or I might brand as fortunate—or perhaps favored is more the word; one of those gents for whom life seems to have aligned and given all that could have been asked of it. And indeed this man *had* counted himself fortunate, regarding both his lot when he came to face his ordeal—in his case as hostage in a bank robbery—and in surviving it. The man had praised Jesus and thanked his lucky stars, but ultimately he was not able to answer my questions as to the general effect of being so-near death for the gent who is satisfied. In fact this fellow—a loose acquaintance at best—did not seem to construct his memories around the *sensations* of incidents atall but rather around his recollections of the facts, and could recount for me only the actions which had transpired, as if reciting the script to a play. From his account I could surmise only that his personal satisfaction had, in that critical moment, served to focus his attentions toward thoughts of his preservation, of that charmed life, thick, as it was, with providence. And yes the fellow did claim some manner of responsibility to pay back, somehow, whatever system it was he held responsible for that providence, but so far as I was able to discern his experience had not produced introspection of much depth nor even altered his succeeding behavior in substance.

But the second subject—a man who, it turned out, had quite-a-few near-misses—had quite a different view on the experience of confronting death entire.

To set the stage:

I came to hear the tale of the Piedmont's Plot while on the long train ride down the mighty gorge of the Columbia River as both this second subject and I were making west toward Portland, in the state of Oregon.

As happens on such long-trips, where amongst strangers the passage of courteous conversation leads to the sharing of stories of increasing intimacy, so it was in this case; the concessions of small bits of personal histories, and the insights such histories provide, wound, eventually, to the outlining of this man's private philosophies then to the recounting of the broader affairs which amalgamated into the tale here-presented (with, shall we say, *complementation* here and there, for the effect of having witnessed it in the person); an account which—to my ears at the least—had marks of import of which the teller seemed hardly aware.

Regardless, it was over this trip that the story of the Piedmont's plot unfolded, told by this peculiarly disappointed saint of a fellow I mention.

Though the man—who was by-this-time well in to, if not leaving, his middle age—began as a stranger to me, what was clear near-immediate was that he had been no fortuned son—though he was by-now in possession of at least some material wealth. And though the certainty of his satisfaction was woven through near-each thread of our conversation, the *source* of that satisfaction, and of the exquisite confidence in his own standing, was difficult, at first, to discern. But as I came to hear this man's stories—of a man face-to ordeal up-on ordeal—and as I attuned myself to their theme, and as I came to realize that here indeed was a requisite man for the conduction of my scientific curiosity, imagine my utter surprise to find, when finally asked just what it is such a requisite might experience in a true moment of final reckoning, that here was a fellow who was *not* compelled toward gratitude, for his fortuned life, of any kind.

Yes, you have read correctly. This one time I met, finally, a man who did exude *utter* satisfaction with the way his life had been lived, and who had credibly confronted, on several occasions, the compelling prospect of his own demise, yet gave hardly the insight I expected: That it is not-at-all bliss nor tranquility, some form of contentment nor even smug self-gratification that the right man should expect to find upon the face of death; despite his righteousness—or perhaps because-of it.

Rather, what I found during the unfolding of his tale over that long train ride was that the sufficient man is perhaps predisposed to suffer a strange and a rather singular condition; that because he *has* lived a decent and a principled life he need not imagine, and so need not idealize, what such a satisfied life might be; so that at its end he knows, somewhat uniquely, there is, simply put, nothing of the 'right' life to be grateful for.

And indeed the stories of my subject, and the tone

in which he conveyed them, may have gone so far as to suggest that at no point would he have even been bitter for the loss of it!

Not to say the man was unsettled. Such was simply not the case. The man was pleasant and courteous and in general behaved as anyone should expect. But at best the man was perhaps what you or I might call *amicable* in these of his ultimate confrontations; that at any of his times, his time might have been up.

His story is one I could never forget.

To this day I can still picture the cracks and crags of the man's face and hear the deep bellow of his voice. I can still conjure images of the pillared walls of the great Gorge of the Columbia as they passed by the windows of our rail car as he was telling. And I can still see the man's sad smiles, his furled brow, and finally the quiet that settled over him as he whittled away the years between him and his memories, and as he put me in connection with them.

How I listened. And how I've re-collected his story over and over because, as I've said, it's rare-enough a man must really confront how he's spent his life and rarer still he finds he's done the right things but it's rarest of all a man arrives at some solid truth he can really share to you; even if that truth is just how cold and bitter, cruel and downright awful a place this world of ours really can be.

Not to spoil the story but perhaps to *fully* preface, the recounting of the events about-to unfold was a revelation to me. Today we stand in the shade of the edifice of a Constitution now grown so old, so common, so formative and so seemingly natural to our safe and

comforted daily American lives we plain forget *why* such
a document needed drafting in the first place. Today's
citizen easily imagines his part in our world to be the
discovery of a better path, an easier way, to live a more
pristine life, to be bolder or kinder or some other thing
in relation to those lives benchmarked by our past. If
we can all be honest we picture our modern selves as
wranglers of some destiny; the pluckers of fruit ripe
from the tree. But step back and examine that a bit.
Imagine, if you can, the view of mighty God and recall,
if you've read the Good Book—or even just heard the
story—the plight of old Job; a man who had everything
that could be asked for, and who lost all of it, and who
then found himself in contemplation on why things
happen the way they do. What I took from this train ride
was insight from a man who *had* come across, though
he did not preach it, just what it is this is all about;
and whose attitude from-such was, as I've mentioned,
nothing more and nothing less than acceptance, of a
general principle life would seem to teach those who
wind up in direct-enough confrontation with it:

Our duty is not to do right. And it could never be
sufficient to 'do the best one can,' or even to be right
in one's own eyes; for failure is failure, whatever one's
intent. At best our part would seem the actor's; to play
our role, blindly following our hidden script, on a stage
bigger than anything we'll ever know. And if God
needed more from us than that, well, he'd a said so.

THE
PLEASANT
PHEASANT

✢

This happening starts, for any intent or purpose, in a
tucked-away corner of the vast interior of the sprawling
American northwest frontier; in a wild-grass valley
of the southern Palouse about half the way along the
Army's old Mullan trail—which to the younger reader
was the military road which ran south from Spokane
through some hundred miles of rolling, grass-covered
hills.

And when I say half the way along I should clarify;
not half-along the entire road, nor half from Spokane,
but halfway from a place called Lyon's Ferry to the
terminus of the trail in Walla Walla (or the other way
around).

Though I have not seen it in the person, the
description of the town here-located, going by-that-time
by the name Prescott, was of little more than a one-
street—but more on that subsequently. For now all that
needs establishing is this dinky café located along that
one street by the name The Pleasant Pheasant, which had

in its heyday been quite a successful operation but which
was by-this-time pretty well done with.

As described, the Pheasant, as it was called in
shorthand, was, though certainly cheap, not without its
charms. The picture I got was of hewn lumber tables
polished soft from so-many-years of scrubbing, a mis-
match of chairs grabbed-from, among other places, a
community church which used-to-be across the street,
and in the windows sun-beat curtains hung thread-bare;
a ceiling, once painted in milk-white, by-now near-black
in spots from the smoke of candles and most definitely
brown in others from years of the kitchen's belchings;
sparse wall-hangings cut-from book illustrations,
paper clippings, or even snippets from the occasional
periodical which found its way into the town; and yet
oddly lavish for somewhere so out-of-the-way—and
perhaps some indication of how popular the place
must have once-been—and this was recounted to me in
detail—the timbers of the walls had been plastered and
then covered in rich brown paper accented with artwork
printed in ink of a royal-purple hue which showed the
diagonal drama of pheasant-after-pheasant taking flight
from angry hunter after angry hunter.

So imagine, with Prescott so out-of-the-way that the
road-weary is coming near-straight-from the wilderness
of a grassland onto this scene of a brick building'd town
in the first place, and then to a glass-fronted café in the
second, upon which the words PLEASANT PHEASANT
are scrolled out in intricate gold-flake; that inside said
road-weary should find the lavishness of walls covered
in decorative paper, in the first place; I imagine such
travelers, though undoubtedly desperate for meal, must
have had at least something of a laugh at seeing that

name, and spelled outside so fancily, and then coming inside to see, with great irony, quite the opposite story scrolled upon the walls!

But the Pheasant had fallen by-this-time out-of the care of its original owner and in-to the care of a remaining descendant; a young woman by the name of Miss Norma Hatcherly who, coming to it through inheritance and not-yet having a man and living with her adopted aunt and uncle only a quarter-mile up the road, had just recently been declared proper by the general townsfolk to tend-to the place.

In fact The Pheasant had only just recently reopened after some time of being closed and so it was only of-late the young Miss Norma had become both cook *and* waitress, though she did apparently have a wash girl on Tuesdays and Thursdays in her younger sister Ida. On this morn, though, it was just Norma and three customers; two acquaintances in the front window booth, in town on some Grange business, and a road-weary huntsman-type sat way back at the two-chair in the far corner, about as far from those windows as one could get—and tucked right up against that gawdy wall-paper.

What follows is, admittedly, in part the product of my machinations; but it is—in fact—based in significant part upon dialogue conveyed to me by the drama's central character:

While those two acquainted Grangemen were, at present, carrying on a boisterous conversation, which was growing louder by the moment, the huntsman was doing quite the opposite and was quietly reading the café's copy of *The Walla Walla Statemen*[1]—not on account of his democratic leanings so much as

1   The name may be just *Walla Walla Stateman*; it has been some time since I last saw a copy—please excuse not knowing the proper title.

on account of there not being Republicans yet in the Prescott valley who took the *Walla Walla Union*—least none who'd leave their expired copies with the café. And it's a curious detail, and I'd've certainly forgiven the man for forgetting it, but though this was in fact the 14th of March[2], the date on the issue in the huntsman's hands read *March the 11th*, 1886.

But, as I'm told, this was life in such a place at such a time: Three-days-old news was 'current nuff' and republican or democrat, reading material passed time the same.

Now the truth of the situation with this huntsman was not quite so simple to the careful observer as it would-have appeared to the casual one. The man certainly did look the part, of a huntsman dropped-by for some breakfast and maybe some respite from his hunt, but for little cues in his dress which offered material hints as to a distinction:

While the usual huntsman's woolies would be plenty smelly, and yes caked in dirt, they'd seldom be of tattered edge or loosened seam. Even so far north, two-days hike from the county seat, huntsmen were by-this-time more for the sport than survival and held their horse-kicked dirt with civility, in upright backs, shined buckles and fresh—if not freshly laundered— warm wear; as this was still only mid-March. And beside, a poor, or a destitute huntsman[3] would simply have no need of paid breakfast and would rather be

---

2   Incidentally I have recently realized this day to have been the seventh birthday of one Albert Einstein, a man who has recently done a thing or two for our understanding of this world.

3   Yes, even back then there remained those who lived their whole lives off the out-of-doors.

by-now enjoying winter grains, quail eggs or, were he
so fortunate as to possess both gun *and* ammunition, the
occasional pheasant; rather than respiting beside a wall
papered in them.

But in *this* huntsman neither the sportsman nor the
have-not were quite the case.

Not to say the man was disheveled. By no means.
His hair was short and his face freshly shaved below
his must-ache. But his buckles, rather than shining,
were shined-*off*. His edges, while not-frayed, were
nonetheless wore-thin so that it was clear that this man
worked in his outdoor dress. And in the *wild* west, still,
of Washington Territory, which was some years yet even
from statehood, and in Prescott, which featured not even
yet the luxe of regular rail service, there was only one
occupation the observant man could expect this hunter
occupied; and which the grangemen, with their bowler
hats and silk-lined jackets, had to assume:

That this was a man who hunted bounty.

And they would have been right.

Not that it troubled, any of them. The man was
pleasant enough. He sipped softly at his coffee and
read quietly his paper and smiled, polite, at the young
Miss Norma and articulated his order in king's-enough
English, for two eggs over medium an two pieces a
toasted bread; and otherwise kept to his own with at-
most the occasional turn of the page of the café's paper.

Unlike those grangemen, who were quite another
story:

Presently *their* talk had turned, as the talks of such
is want to do, to 'these days' and the almost-always-
alarming 'signs of the times.' At this particular moment
the latest in the unending onslaught on civilization

was the coming scourge of electricity and how, though there would be much promised material luxury, these coming luxes would surely turn the next generation into impotent milksops. This, these grangemen had decided, was a surety which was absolutely *not* to be abided:

"Say, Miss Norma," the elder of the two was shouting halfway across the place, "lemme ask you, do you have inclination toward replacing wood n candle?"

And "What's this?" Norma shouted back from behind the washroom curtain before she could emerge.

"We're askin," the younger filled in, "what's yer thoughts on the matter a modernization? Do you have opinion as to whether it should be coal n gas gets brought up here to the valley or you think it should be lectricity?"

"What is that?" Norma finally asked, serious. "I been hearin bout it more n more in here, but I don't know exactly what ... e·lectricity is."

The younger of the grangemen leaned forward.

"Either way you don't gotta go out an fine chopped wood for yer heater, but in the one case you replace yer candles with lights run off gas from a line an yer heat off a coal hopper, an in the other ya just flip a lever an light comes on auto·matic."

Now I imagine the young Miss Hatcherly must have thought on this a moment, still in the doorway to the wash closet.

"Well," she finally did say, "in the first case I ain't allowed to keep open past dark anyhow, so the only time we burn candles anymore is maybe on a real cloudy day."

And then she chewed a nail as she thought on it
somemore.

"But I suppose, were it me still around, after I get
married off, an still tendin here, it sounds much simpler
to flip a lever than what I hear bout gas lamps."

And the elder of the grangemen leaned back and his
eyes grew wide.

"See!" the man near-shouted, "Exactly my point!
Electrification is sure to cause damage to the future
generation. How can they turn it down?"

And the man scanned the otherwise-empty room and
even caught the quick glance of the huntsman from just
above the page of his paper.

"How *could* they say no?" the elder wagged his
finger at the younger, "And that day is coming *when a
young man will not even know how to chop a tree!*"

But "Oh," the younger came back. "No one could
forget how to chop a tree. It couldn't be simpler."

But the elder retorted:

"You mark my words! We face a choice, though you
may be too young to appreciate it; at some point it will
be realized that we ought to have started turning down
these new conveniences, for our very own benefaction!"

"Well sure but that's a ways off."

"Not long enough from the sound of it."

And it was here, finally, after near-half-an-hour
of this, the huntsman had enough. He shook his paper
suddenly closed, so he had their attention, though he
then took a long, upturned sip of his coffee, then sat it
down gingerly and then, finally, turned in their direction.

"Ya know," he boomed, his voice strong for how
gentle he'd been careful to remain until then, "bout half

a decade ago, I believe it's been, I had occasion, on
business--"

But then he looked suddenly to Miss Norma, then
back to these gentlemen.

"Hope I'm not interruptin..."

"Not at all," the elder grangeman finally gave.

"Apologize if I had," the huntsman replied, "Just
thought I'd offer a, observation."

Then he moved his chair back a little, to better afford
himself the turn to face them.

"Several years back," he started again, "I had
occasion, on some business, to take the *Columbia*
up from San Fran. Now she was the first vessel ta be
lectrically outfitted with lightin, if ya didn't know. N-fact
twas Mister Edison himself who undertook the task, as I
understan it.

"Now yer experiences with lectricity sound ta me
ta be second han, so I thought it might be useful to ya
ta hear a first-han account. An gentlemen lemme tell ya,
that stuff worked-a-charm!"

"That so," the elder grangeman replied.

And the huntsman nodded his head.

"The novelty! A walkin upon her deck after hours,
way out on the open waters, on a night so dark you'd
otherwise think yer eyes was shut. An yet, upon that
deck, the full brightness of almost daylight?" The
huntsman shook his head. "I thought, an gentlemen this
was five years ago; I thought, now *here's* the future. An,
uh, pardon the… expression, but it will almost certainly
be a bright one."

To this the elder grangeman smiled but then set back
in his padded bench and crossed his arms, to defend

himself:

"With all due respect sir, that the future will be one of tremendous, even luxurious utility is not in doubt. Why, I hear the application of electricity will be manifold; well... beyond the imaginations of us here in this café.

"Supposedly, in time, electrification will extend into the field of medicine, and if the speculation is correct, some day we may even be able to cheat death, through electrical reanimation. And yes," and here the grangeman turned and nodded to Miss Norma, "I know this-all sounds quite incredible, but these things are the coming tide of a future completely unlike the one speculated on by even one or two generations proceeding us. But again, with all due respect, that the future will be bright is *not* what I'm arguin. What I argue is that the spectacular *ease*, of yes even a thing as simple as throwing a lever to bring upon light, will so *alter* us, and in fact *baby* us in its luxury, that over time our ... daftness will become a... *cost*, so expensive as to... no longer be in our own interest."

"Oh now!" the huntsman came back, "What about steam? Sir, we've heard this argument before! But... taking you for grangemen?"

They both nodded.

"You then work with the farmer? An even now are the farmers not reapin the benefits a industry?"

And here Norma, who felt (I imagine) it was likely time to return to her dishes, would've quickly interjected toward the huntsman, "Lemme getcha somemore coffee."

"I'd oblige."

"Look," the elder grangeman carried on, "I am no luddite. I do not... pre-tend the notion that progress is avoidable. But sir, electrification is distinct. The application of steam was one of industrial praxis. The locomotive, the tractor, the drill, the factory power plant; these are all implements of *industry*."

Norma poured fresh coffee, from the pot, into the huntsman's upheld mug.

"I thank you."

"But electricity," the elder continued, "apart from entering, and yes sometimes improving *industrial* application, has set its sights upon entering *our very homes*!"

And the elder cast a glance in Norma's direction as she disappeared behind the curtain.

"Now, where electricity can turn the power of one man into the output of five, say; or yes, in context of your suggestion that it might offer to the farmer the multiplication of yields, then unquestionably; our future will invariably be a bright one, full of manifold advances. But the fact is alongside such benefits I, and I am hardly alone here, foresee a cost potentially much greater in, as I've been saying, it will cause us to lose, In Our Young, OVER TIME, THEIR... VERY... MASTERY OF THE WORLD!"

And here the elder grangeman's face had become quite red and he was forced to take respite in a drink of water, presumably to cool himself.

"Look" the huntsman offered, "sirs, with all due respect, I never had occasion to matriculate to no college, as I'm sure you-all have, so, understood, I concede, you likely have me bested so far's expertise.

"But... to put it plain..."

And here the huntsman became quiet a moment; and then, softly:

"I too... have seen things, gentlemen."

And then he stopped and just stared a moment, with his nose down toward the floor so his eyes peaked out low from under his brow.

"As you may have ascertained from my attire I am a man who makes his way... in a particular trade, which I won't discuss," he nodded toward the washroom curtain, "in the company a the young woman, but I think yall can guess the trade."

Both men nodded.

"It does afford me, upon quite regular occasion, a... glance, if ya will, hind the... curtain, if ya will, as ta the inner workins a... the *will* of a man."

And the elder stared, and even the younger was turned to look behind him.

"So I do feel this qualifies me ta speak toward this regard."

Finally the elder grangeman shrugged and then offered a conciliatory nod, so the huntsman continued.

"Not insight, mind ya, inta what a man says'e wants or how itis weall'll *claim* we conduct ourselves, in the circumstance a bein roun *other* men."

And here the huntsman took a quick swig of his coffee.

"Not how weall claim we *would* act; but how it is a man *does* act. How it is he *does* conduct'imself, when'e's on'is own. Or--"

And he was surprised to catch Norma peaking out from behind her curtain.

"My apologies miss," he said, but then returned to

these grangemen, "but how it is a man, truthfully, *does*
conduct'imself, when'e actually faces'is end.

"...when'e faces, very di·rect·ly, the prospect of'is
own demise."

And the two grangemen, and for that matter the
young Ms. Hatcherly had, simply put, no reply with
which to fill the un-settling gap the huntsman here-
left in the conversation; by grabbing again his mug
and bringing it gentle up-to his lips, and by taking yet
another slow, simmering sip of his coffee as he stared,
unrelenting, into the eyes of the elder-of-these-two
grangemen.

But at last to this stare the elder grangeman took it as
his duty to respond:

"Would you doubt," the grangeman said, "sir, that
the young man, who has had, for as long as there have
been young men, to learn to turn the land or to swing
the axe or whathaveyou... that losing such ability will
nodoubt leave us in a position which is not to be aspired
to?"

And the huntsman, who in fact had been interrupted,
did think on that a moment.

And then he did reply:
"Well, ta finish my thought:
"Man will *always* find a way... ta survive. I know
this from experience. An if he can *not* find a way he'll
look, an'e won't stop lookin; fer *any* way ta survive, so
far as it is possible to'im. … Until…"

And here, as was usual when he spoke on matters
related to the insights afforded by his career, the

huntsman found himself faced-to the diverted eyes of
both the café's lady and the younger grangeman. But he
still had the attention of the *elder*, and the conversation
was started, so he figured he'd end it.

But then he thought again.

"As I think on it..." the huntsman said instead, "I
might be inclined, given maybe a little more thought...
that a young man's hardly challenged, by learnin ta till, r
ta chop... r ta harvest."

And as the huntsman wondered if he had complete-
enough a position to draw some helpful conclusion he
took a breath and he exhaled, but careful, so-as not to
give the impression he might be frustrated or annoyed.

"Not ta... o·ffend, but this lectricity these brilliant
inventors and the like've unlocked: *Learnin bout the
mysteries a the forces hind lightnin in the clouds...* Might
that not be more... fittin to us? Than the challenge a
learnin the simplicities a everyday survival?"

"--not ta say ya ain't right," the huntsman quickly
interjected, "I do see where ya come from. An we *are*
well ta harden ourselves. ...but maybe there'll be new
hardnins, in the face a those new luxuries the future
seems it'll be offerin, we ain't even fathomed yet."

And then the huntsman shrugged.

And then the elder grangeman shrugged.

And then the hunter, suddenly aware of the time,
thought to pull his watch from his jacket pocket and to
check it. And it was nearly nine and the huntsman knew
he'd better be getting along.

"Perhaps you're right," the elder grangeman did give
back. And our huntsman just looked at him a moment
as he tucked his pocket watch back away, then smiled

polite.

"Who really knows," the huntsman at-last replied.
Then he turned to the young woman:

"Miss," he said, with a different kind of smile, "that
was a fine meal you cooked, an I greatly appreciate it.
Thank you, kindly."

And then he produced his billfold from his inner
pocket and pulled from-it a crisp one-dollar bill and he
set it down on the table in her view.

"Will a dollar be sufficient?"

"Oh that will be more than sufficient sir. Thank
you!"

"Excellent coffee by the way," he said, then stood,
then slipped his billfold back inside, "An I thank you for
bein open on a Sunday." Then he took his wide-brimmed
cow hat and placed it upon his head, and then he turned
to the other two men.

"Gentlemen," he said, "I hope I have not disturbed
your meal."

"Not at all," the elder grangeman responded, "Not at
all. It was a pleasure," and the elder offered his hand, but
did remain seated.

And the huntsman took the few steps to him,
accepted the hand, firmly, and gave a shake.

"Fare well."

"Farewell."

And even the younger grangeman muttered, "Good
bye."

THE SHERIFF
BRAINERD DICE

✢

As was alluded earlier, in those days the town of Prescott had just the one kept street, which was then-called Spalding Street after a Reverend Spalding who'd first settled a property there with intent to share civility to the natives. And Spalding crossed, north-to-south, a west-to-east portion of the aforementioned great Mullan Trail—which, to refresh, was the long wagon trail built by the U.S. Army a quarter-century prior for the facilitation of expansion by settlers into the northwest interiors of the vast Dakota and Oregon territories, before those territories were further split into the Idaho, Montana, and Washington territories we-all remember today.

Around this intersection, though, the Mullan trail was here-called, by the locals at least, the Dayton Road, as the road here-ran up the Prescott Valley all the way out to Waitsburg and then to Dayton beyond.

But back to Spalding Street:

At this time one familiar with the town would have expected to find along Spalding buildings housing both the local Grange *and* the more-recent Farmer's Cooperative, a newly installed Post Office, and the two-story Harper Building on the ground floor of which the aforementioned Pleasant Pheasant neighbored with the Prescott General Store. One may *not*, however, have expected to come-across the building newly-raised across-from the Harper, on the westerly corner and atop the remains of that aforementioned first Community Church; a new construction put up only over the summer and fall before, and in brick no-less; Frank Clague's Prescott Hotel.

This handsome erection, with tall glass front windows and spacious lobby below its second floor, and striking white trim against the red of its brick and in the sashes of its windows, was where our huntsman had been instructed, by electrical telegraph no-less, to report for his day's business.

And so it was that he crossed the recent gravel of Spalding Street careful, to avoid the mud that showed-through here-and-there, as he'd be entering that Hotel's lobby dirty enough without more filth on his boots.

Inside he was greeted quite warmly by Isabella Clague, whom he'd heard recent mention of as Mr. Clague's second wife. And he approached the counter she was seated behind, filing her nails, with a nod and then in a soft french voice he got, "You must be looking for zeh Sher·iff."

"Yes. Thank you ma'am."

"He's up zeh stairs, in room too-oh-too."

"Much obliged."

That the huntsman should find Mrs. Clague fetching was not a surprise to him. But what did surprise was

the soothing quality of her voice, which took him quite
unexpected; and perhaps in concert with having so-
recently conversed with the young Ms. Hatcherly, he
found suddenly that he longed for the smooth skin and
the soft features of the female. But being on business
he hid these thoughts, even from himself, and aimed
himself for the stairway immediate, and did not grant
himself even a glance back at the fair face or the clean
hair of Mrs. Clague, so her beauty would imprint no
further upon him.

For now was not the time.
Now was the time for work.
And it was not long before the huntsman, whose
name's Isaac by the way, was up those stairs and to a
sky-window-lit upper hallway done in fresh pine, and
before he found his door, and before he rapped upon it.
And "Yes!" came a hoarse old voice from the door's
other side.
"This the room a the Sheriff?"
"Is today. Come inside."
And the huntsman found the door unlocked, and
did, open it, and did come inside, and was soon face-to
a man ten or could-be twenty years his senior, seated
at a desk very near the door; a man with near-white
facial gruff below his mustache and a head so-balded
as to near-isolate a button of hair mid-forehead; but
nonetheless hair long and smooth and so-conditioned as
to be flowing.
"You must be my bountyman."
The huntsman nodded.
"Well good. How were yer travels?"
"Fine."

"Glad ta hear it," the Sheriff gave, but the while the
man sorted through a mess of papers stacked before him
on his desk.

"Which way'd ya come?"

"Outta Walla Walla, long the Hart road."

To this the Sheriff nodded, then stopped, then looked
up from his papers and over the man, then back to the
mess upon his desk; then sorted somemore. But the
still-standing huntsman was expecting to be asked to sit,
and had not yet so-been; and so, as he waited, and as this
sheriff sifted still, the huntsman thought to carry on the
conversation.

"I understand," the huntsman said, and did have the
other man's attention, "the bounty in question is three-
hundred dollars?"

"That's right," the Sheriff answered then finally
pulled a Wanted poster from his stack and set it on top
with some relief.

And as our hunter had expected, this Wanted paper
matched the one he himself held, folded up in his inner
jacket's pocket, hid even beneath his billfold.

But the Sheriff continued his search, through
his papers, and the hunter guessed it must be for the
remainder of the forms necessary to commence a hunt;
so he waited, and as he did he examined, again, and
thorough, the face sketched upon that Wanted paper.

It was a face he found curious because it was a
sketch of less detail than the usual he encountered; of
distinct line and not-at-all the normal small flits of lines,
from an artist who either knew the face of the hunted
already or who was not inclined toward accuracy in
this instance. And it was this which truly gathered the

huntsman's attention, and it was the answer to which he was most anxious to get from this Sheriff. For the boy in the picture couldn't've been more than eighteen at most or fifteen at least, and was certainly *not* his usual bounty.

But as he believed he'd waited long-enough for the silence to grow uncomfortable, and with this Sheriff still stopping, periodic, to read this-or-that of his papers, the huntsman again interjected:

"So what *can* you tell me? …bout the hunted?"

And the Sheriff looked up again and smiled apologetic and then appeared to give-up his search and instead leaned back in his chair and let out a long, frustrated sigh. Then the man dug around in the woolen pocket of his handsome sheriff's jacket until he produced from-it a sturdy glossed pipe which looked to be in mahogany entire save for just a delicate lip of ceramic on the mouthpiece.

And then, finally, pipe-in-his-hand, the Sheriff began:

"How familiar are you, with the valley here?"

And then he pulled out a match and lit his pipe as the huntsman began his answer.

"I'm familiar. Least somewhat." the hunter replied. "I chased two bandits through in seventy-nine. Fled up the Snake then headed down the valley here makin for the mountains."

And the Sheriff suckled his pipe the while.

"Shot em both outside the Anchor Saloon in Waitsburg. Fellas could not say no to a drink, s how I got em. Killed the one on that spot. Chased the other clear ta Dayton fore *he* finally felled."

And the Sheriff nodded and his eyebrows raised up.

"Anyhow," the hunter continued, "come right through here. Ate at the Pheasant in-fact, even way back then."

And the Sheriff nodded. "I believe I heard-bout that hunt. The Baker boys?"

"This' the Chester brothers. Harry an Ben."

"S what I meant."

And the huntsman nodded, though he doubted the Chester brothers truly were who the Sheriff meant. But the huntsman continued:

"I just come-from the Pheasant, just now. Owner's gone?"

The Sheriff nodded, "Believe she died last year."

Another puff.

"Fever."

And again the huntsman nodded. This *was* what he'd heard.

And the Sheriff worked his pipe's stuffings somemore, into a glowing ember, then suckled deep and then bellowed a thick cloud of smoke.

And then he looked back to his huntsman.

"Lemme gitcha chair."

The Sheriff rose, thick-of-frame as he was, and disappeared into the anteroom. And then he came back a moment later with a tall-back dining chair and set it down across from his desk, just inside the door. And then he closed the door behind the hunter then repositioned the chair a little farther away and then made motion for his hunter to take his seat at last, then sat down himself, again across-from, and opposite, his man.

"So," the Sheriff finally started, "West, --r scuse me, east a town, down the river oh maybe halfway to the confluence, up ta yer north; that's the Piedmont place."

"Ta the north?" the huntsman asked. "Thought I come in *past* Piedmont's."

"From the South?"

The hunter nodded.

The Sheriff thought on this and then with a sheepish grin did nod too. "Ya did," he chuckled as he realized the trouble, "Cross from the Hart property? That's Piedmont's homestead. In oat?"

"Looked like."

"Yep. Up ta the *north*, that's Piedmont's *plot*. Four hunred acres, supposed to go inta wheat next month."

And the Sheriff struggled to rise from his seat, then made his way over to the nearest of the tall windows of the Prescott Hotel, and then the man looked down upon Spalding Street below and then out overtop the Post Office and on down the valley.

"It's prime land," he finally gave, then turned back to the huntsman.

"Hector Piedmont's workin ta wrangle it from the Lowrey's since at least seventy-six with the idea, a late, a giftin it as'is daughter's dowry."

"Kay," the hunter said.

"Well…" the Sheriff said, then took another puff, then turned back to look upon the view some-more. Then the man blew smoke out his nostrils. "…as a last Tuesday, from the sound of it, Piedmont's come up dead."

"Oh," the huntsman replied, then leaned back in his chair, now-clear on where he came into this. Then the huntsman leaned forward, took his finger and dropped it square on the nose of the face upon that Wanted poster.

"An this' the one who did it?"
"His son-in-law."

This caught our huntsman off his guard. He leaned
back in his chair again, his eyes a little wide.
And the Sheriff took another puff off his pipe and
blew somemore smoke in the morning light and just
looked out the window a while.

"So," the hunter finally gave, "ya cain't find'im?"
But the Sheriff shook his head.
"Ain't that. I know where'e is."
And the Sheriff took yet another puff. "He's hangin
aroun the pro·per·ty."
And this had our huntsman genuinely perplexed.

"He won't come out?"
"He'll come. I don't xpect much struggle."

"So…" the huntsman finally gave, but then paused.
Then, finally, "…why…
"…the bounty?"
And it was then that the Sheriff turned to face his
man, and then the Sheriff smiled; one of those knowing
smiles, where a man's eyes wrinkle up and would seem
to tell you the whole story, only in their own way; to
where you can't get at it quite. And in this case adding
to the mystery, those wrinkled eyes weren't quite in
agreement with what it was this sheriff's downturned
mouth was also saying; which was maybe more regret
than his sly eyes cared to betray. But then the Sheriff
spoke again.
"Walla Walla County," he began, "is a county a

considerable size. An now you likely took notice we ain't meetin in the local de·pu·tee's office. N fact yer prolly inclined ta wonder why it is yer talkin ta the Sheriff atall an *not* that local depudee."

"Certainly curious."

The Sheriff nodded and smiled again, but more a conciliatory smile this time, in acknowledgment, it seemed, of just how un-usual this-all indeed was.

"Well," the Sheriff gave, pipe-in-his-hand, "the short of it is, this place ain't got, a deputy—which might seem an oversight but this…" and he motioned toward the windows and even chuckled a little, "is about the dullest piece a land, from the perspective a the law anyhow, I think there ever was.

"Do you know I've had all a two complaints up north here since I come out west ta work law in… oh… bout sixty eight? One's a drunk, husband, tryin ta cheat on'is wife, an the other turned out an errant receipt down here at the local Grange."

Then the Sheriff took a quick puff then let the smoke slip out his mouth as he continued.

"Now am I rememberin you was once a man a the law yerself?"

The huntsman nodded.

"Tried deputizin, out in Five Valleys."

"That's Missoula county?"

"Thereabouts. But I missed travelin."

"Road always wore me out personally," the Sheriff said, "Got bad knees." And then he pointed down to them, as if the hunter didn't know what knees was.

"Anyhow," the Sheriff carried on, "as a lawman then—an maybe *more* as a man fer bouny—ya understan the need fer law ain't necessarily when 'all's civil,' as a feller might, but rather when one gets those glances a… *incivility*." And the Sheriff seethed this last word.

"Mosta the time," he quickly continued, "fer our type, it's our privilege ta see the world in the raw, as ya might. But fer these folk, lucky fer them, civility is really the only thing they've ever known."

And then he took yet another pull from his pipe.

"Fer them it's all… chain yer beasts, till yer soil, get the harvest then… dos-à-doe. Their whole lives r built roun gettin long ya know. Social callin, dances down at the Grange hall…" he shrugged, "get yer church in n that's… bout it."

He took a breath.

"Life fer these folk ain't what we've seen it ta properly be."

The hunter nodded.

"Fer them it's… all of it… just git along, do yer plowin, an jist…"

And again the pipe was at the man's lips.

"…watch as the things grow."

And again this Sheriff took a pull.

A long one.

Which he then blew out in a series of small clouds that came to surround him and caught in the window light and bathed him in a cool blue haze which became quite striking.

"But," the man finally continued, "at least in my experience, while we harsher lads have ta… fight, pon more'n o·ccasion, ta keep back the savage should frequent the gate, isn't til ya come to a place like this;

these quiet, simple, little… utopias, that--"

"Utopias?" the hunter interrupted, earnest in his unfamiliarity with the word, and the Sheriff took him strange a moment.

"Ever read Sir Thomas Moore?" the Sheriff finally asked.

"I have not," the hunter had to say.

And the Sheriff smiled again, polite.

"Never mind then."

He took another quick pull then turned back and looked out his window again.

"What I'm reminded, when I come to a place such-as, is that yes we do have ta fight fer our peace. But that … civility, we intend t'afford is not, as one might think, some thing a man can jist … grab a hold a.

"smore like sand," the Sheriff said, and he held his hand out, his fingers curled, "ta where if ya ain't careful it'll slip right through yer fingers."

And the hunter caught himself just watching, the occasion of this speech, which was, he was realizing, quite a spectacle.

The Sheriff continued.

"So when David Lowey give away—an I don't mean give *away* so much as give *up* maybe—a *sizable* plot so Hector Piedmont's only daughter can be afforded a dowry for her marriage to Lowrey's eldest boy, that there, sir, is a whole lotta civility goin roun."

And then, finally, the Sheriff turned from his window, yes took another puff, but at last the man took his seat; and his chair creaked under his heavy load.

And then the man crossed his legs and then, at last, looked our hunter in the eye.

And then he carried on.

"It's not unlike a waltz, the way these people operate up here. An so when that eldest, *Constance* Lowrey," and he pointed to the flyer, "shoots'is father-in-law-ta-be in the back, what we're facin is not quite the simple *crime* upon which the application a justice is ta be swiftly an simply applied. Inotherwords this' *not* the clean matter-a-the-law a victim-n-assailant that it may at-first appear.

"Pardon if this seems a tad fac·ile but this-all up here's more akin to a formal, as-in a ball, r a dance; s what I meant by the waltz… Any how, here in the middle a all this… extravaganza, someone's jist been derogated; an if we ain't real careful, right infrona eerybody."

And again the Sheriff looked our hunter dead in the eye.

And the hunter supposed he took the man's meaning.

Just seemed an odd way to put it.

But the Sheriff took another of his puffs and let another of his clouds engulf him and it was from within this cloud that he continued.

"Left unanswered, everything'd come to a halt an eerybody'd jist crane their necks an they'd all jist kinda end up … waitin ta see what it is gonna happen next."

"I mean," the Sheriff quickly added, "I respect, an regret, the lossa Hector's life. But that's personal. But so far's the townsfolk's concerned? What I guess ya gotta appreciate's, the law out here ain't what *we* know it ta properly be. It ain't the … waiver you'r I use ta commit our violences—necessary though those violences may be. Fer these folk, the law is…

"It's their… customs. The customs a their… dance, is, I guess, the best way I know how ta put it."

And the Sheriff again looked to our hunter.

And our hunter nodded in reply, clear, enough anyhow, what it was this Sheriff meant for him to get.

"Ta these people," the Sheriff kept on, "the law ain't really more'n a ritual ya know. They don't understan it. They ain't so much as read it. I mean a few have. Bill Perkin's once a lawyer but … I think he's got the only copy a the County Code tween the Snake an the Dayton courthouse."

The man drew a quick puff.

"But anyhow, with one a their own's been killed this is not just a legal matter. Whole families hang in the balance, an if we ain't real careful how we as the law… As host, if ya would; er as proprietor maybe… If we are not real careful they'll all jist, stop keepin ta this dance a theirs, fore they even realize that … dance's what makes life out here work in the first place."

And again the hunter nodded.

"You need an outside party."

The Sheriff nodded.

"I need an outside party."

The hunter nodded more.

"I see that."

And the Sheriff nodded back.

And then the hunter leaned forward, as if to stand.

"So," he asked, "where's'e holed up?"

But the Sheriff leaned back again in his struggling chair and took a slower pull of his pipe—which, in conversations such, meant the hunter had not-quite-yet heard the story entire.

"Well, first off, we have not-yet let on that Hector's dead."

"Oh," the huntsman said, then settled back into his own chair.

"So far as I am able," the Sheriff sighed, "I'd like to turn this thing public a done deal."

"Ah," the hunter replied.

And the Sheriff pulled again off his pipe.

"Ranch hand come down from the hill an come ta me di·rect. Rode south straight off an did not use the telegraph. Now I know this fella, an the man asked fer me personal. *He* saw the murder first-han, an the accused knows'e did, witness it first-han."

And then the Sheriff paused and pressed his pipe to his lips, then drew in deep, and then held it.

And then finally he let it out, and smoke once-again engulfed him.

"We-all know what that means," the Sheriff gave from behind his cloud. "I knew it the moment I heard it. An Constance knows it too. He knows what he done, whatever the reason. An'e knows what the consequence'll be. So I spect he's spendin his time careful, in contemplation."

And then the Sheriff was quiet a spell.

And then he looked back up to his hunter.

"No boy's ever gonna be good-nuff for Hector an'is sweet Narcissa," and the Sheriff shook his head. *"But that man did allow himself ta become outright irrational*! Specially when the mood come upon'im. An while I cain't condone what Constance done, it has not taken me by surprise neither. An where I might feel fer the boy, an were it I who were Judge I might be inclined toward leniency, *the Code a the Territory has clear words bout murder!*"

And the Sheriff nodded to himself, as if he'd convinced himself.

"So all ta say, there's a decency necessary here, I hope ya can appreciate, in how it-is we obtain the boy, never-mind how it-is we come ta bring'im ta justice; cause ya better believe eery one a these folk'll be lookin south ta see what it is justice has ta say; but in the meantime there's four hunred acres ta fall fallow we don't get a lasso on this."

And this last line confused our hunter a little; whatall four hundred fallow acres might have to do with justice; and he did keep his eye on this Sheriff; as the man puffed his smoke somemore, and as he appeared to be thinking on some other angle to the events unfolding.

And as the hunter thought on it he wondered if he'd heard right about the Piedmont girl:

"Piedmont's got no sons?"

"Not a one. An'e lost'is other two daughters."

"How?"

"I believe the one drowned, several years back. The other, fever, as memory serves, an more recent. An now…" and the Sheriff again shook his head, "… Constance won't even be able ta step in fer Missus Piedmont."

Perhaps, the hunter thought, this was the angle troubling the Sheriff so.

"Does she know?" the hunter asked.

But the Sheriff kept shaking his head.

"Not even she."

And then the Sheriff found solace in his pipe again,

which was giving less smoke; and then added:

"Hector n Constance're expected ta be camped up on the plot til week's end."

Another pull, and then, regretful, the Sheriff turned to the hunter:

"…ta prepare the bride's new homestead."

But the hunter just looked on this Sheriff.

"An Constance has not come down?" the hunter finally asked.

"Not so far as I've yet heard. Least as a my most recent information."

"Why not?"

But the Sheriff did not answer immediate. Rather he put his pipe once-again to his lips, ready for more smoke.

But then, rather, he did speak.

"I'm not… quite sure."

And then he pulled.

"Maybe shame?" the Sheriff offered with a shrug and then let the smoke pour from his lips.

"Maybe fear?"

"But he's expectin somebody?" the hunter asked.

"If'e's smart."

Then the Sheriff blew some little rings with what smoke remained in his lungs, and the hunter watched as the last of the rings rolled itself gone then looked down again at the Wanted paper on the Sheriff's desk.

"How old? Is the accused?"

"Nineteen."

"What's'e like?"

The Sheriff shook his head.

"Bright kid. I ain't seem'im since, oh, bout fifteen; but strong, good head on'is shoulders. Not terrible rash."

The hunter nodded.

"An the bride-ta-be?"

"Sixteen. Fresh as a blossom, an still on the homestead."

"Where do they school?" the hunter asked next. And the Sheriff drew in one of those winded breaths, of a man who's taken in too much tobacco and whose lungs have-not-got, for the moment, room enough for good air.

"Home," he finally gave, "They test in Waitsburg though. There's no district out here yet. That's expected once the rail come through."

The huntsman nodded. "Kay" he said then drew a breath of his own. Then he looked back to the Sheriff.

"So," he said, then the hunter leaned forward again, to stand. "Bring'im here? Ride'im south?"

But the Sheriff did not respond. Rather the man set to working the remaining glow in his pipe into yet another ember and made somemore smoke with the rest of his tampings.

And then once-again he exhaled, and a grand cloud of smoke once-again engulfed him.

But he did not say a word.

Rather he just set there and thought.

Or perhaps stewed is more the term.

And then the smoke gradually did clear and the
Sheriff set there still, his eyes locked on our bounty man.

And then, finally, he decided.

And then he nodded.

"Ride'im south."

The hunter nodded.

The Sheriff nodded again. So the hunter thought to
review thisall in his head, and he seemed to have it: Ride
out, quiet, gather the kid, drive him south, without eyes
on him if possible—so maybe over the ridges instead of
down the roads—and deliver him to the Justice of the
county seat.

It was all sound.

Let the townsfolk or the newspapers or whomever
decide what to do with the story, and the questions.
Though there was one remaining item, for the hunter at
least.

"The poster," he said, "reads dead-r-alive."

And the Sheriff nodded. "Preferably alive. I ain't
gotta tell ya that."

And that seemed to conclude it. And the hunter went
to stand, but then the Sheriff added:

"Though… were he *not* ta make it to'is trial? I
suppose those fields could go inta wheat all the sooner."

And the hunter was, all-of-a-sudden, off-put by
this Sheriff and his careless remark. The justice of
the gun had never been his preference, despite—or
perhaps because-of—his occupation. But, he thought,
this business was not his. So he did finally rise up and
straightened his jacket and then slipped his hand inside
his inner pocket to check his copy of the Wanted paper
was still inside, behind his billfold, which was behind his
Colt. Then, once again, he turned to this Sheriff.

"What happens ta the land?"

"Oh…" the elder leaned back in his chair, "it'll go back ta the Lowrey's I spect. I still ain't seen the contract proper. I was only caught up on the whole arrangement myself jist this morn," and the Sheriff motioned to his stack of papers. "Just got the dispatch. Followed me up from the lawyer."

Then the Sheriff himself stood with a grunt.

"I expect," the man muttered, then stepped back over toward the window, then tapped his pipe into the ashtray set on the window sill, "…the Lowrey's'll do their duty ta Missus Piedmont." And then he turned to his hunter and then, with a chuckle:

"Prolly they'll offer their next-a-kin fer the whole lot!"

"Kay" the hunter shrugged. It was no concern of his. He reset his hat, looked out at the clouded sky and then down what he could make of the long valley, and then he tipped his hat to the Sheriff.

"Welp," he said, "I better git to it. What can ya tell me on the lay a the land?"

The Sheriff nodded and then turned back to the window to illustrate.

"Ya see where the Pepper Creek runs down inta the Too-she, down here?"

The huntsman nodded.

"The plot is east a Pepper Creek. You'll ride north, up two berms. On top sounds like there's a shelter on the overlook. Views clear out ta Dayton an the foothills. Beautiful property s what I hear."

"Sounds like."

"That's where you'll find the body. An I expect that's where you'll find the bereaved Master Lowrey."

"Kay," the hunter said. "Oh, an a description?"

"Well, Hector's the one that's dead."

The Sheriff smiled.

"The Lowrey boy."

"I know… He's tall. Prolly six foot. Sandy hair. No left arm."

"Oh," the hunter said, "That's easy!"

"Lost it uner a horse. Had ta be *cut* off," the Sheriff said.

But the huntsman had to wonder why such was not mentioned on the Wanted paper.

"Make'im tough?"

"Imagine so."

The hunter took a breath, stretched his legs, then his neck. "Kay," he finally said, then noticed the Sheriff collecting his own things into an attaché.

"You ain't stickin roun?"

"Nope," the Sheriff said. "Jist came ta be current." Then the man looked up, "Jist wan-ed a be sure a yer arrival. I'm ridin back after lunch."

"Eatin at the Pheasant?"

The Sheriff looked up again.

"You know anywhere else?"

The hunter shook his head.

"I do not."

"Then the Pleasant Pheasant it is."

The hunter nodded, then offered his hand.

"In that case, enjoy. An think a Genevieve for me."

The Sheriff took the hunter's hand and did shake it.

"I will son. An good luck."

BACK TO WORK

✢

At this point the town of Prescott had only recently taken its name, from a C. H. Prescott who was at-that-time a railroad foreman with the Oregon Railway and Navigation Company and who had secured some land nearby the town through his position with that Company's railroad, and who had thought to name *some* place after himself in a bid to convince the Company to locate railroad shops and a water tank nearby for C. H. to oversee.

See the town only ever served two purposes to any degree and would have otherwise died away were it not that it had purposed first as a half-way stop of this segment of the aforementioned Mullan Trail—halfway being half the way between Lyon's Ferry and the old Fort at Walla Walla—back when a fort meant more in relation to the threat posed by the natives—and now, second, as a stop along that rail road as its tracks were being made for Dayton's wheat.

It may also here help to elucidate that while those local to the City of Walla Walla, which occupies very-near the southern border of its presiding County, often

refer to Prescott as being 'in the north,' or *to* the north, or
just The North, Prescott is, in fact, located very near the
geographical center of Walla Walla County. But between
the City and the northernly Town lie only miles and
miles of grass-covered hill and beyond Prescott to the
north only miles and miles more of the same, clear up
to the north-most edge of the County along the cliffs of
the Snake River, up at the aforementioned Lyon's Ferry.
And yet though this northern border is again as far from
Prescott as Prescott from its county's seat, to those in
and around Walla Walla there was little difference. It was
all just North.

In truth the town of Prescott had never much
mattered to the folk of Walla Walla. Rather, the Walla
Wallan would be more concerned with goings-on in
equidistant Pendleton—which was more Walla Walla's
equal but being almost directly south was more properly
along the emigrant's path of the old Oregon Trail.
Rather, the town of Prescott was considered more-oft
in the context of further-east Dayton, in neighboring
Columbia County, which had quickly become a major
settlement for grain, and toward-which the railroad was
at-that-time steadily progressing.

And finally, that Prescott had been platted only four
years prior to the 1886 goings-on of this part of our story
is one of those strange twists fate so-oft hands down: C.
H. Prescott won his battle, for a town in his name, only
to lose at his war. His railway shops, though built quick,
were removed *already by this time*—just four years
hence—to a town a little farther to the north by the name
Starbuck; though Prescott-the-town—soon-after-which
the man himself removed—still clung-to his name, just
as Prescott-the-man still clung-to his land; for a few

more years at least.

So yes the town of Prescott was along the rails but the town was, nonetheless, not yet *served* by rail at that time. Rather until the railroad reached fully to Dayton the road's Company did not see the line as fit for service and so did not even conduct maintenance nor send work trains for the expansion during the winter, which was just-now drawing to a close. And so even though the tracks ran through it—or past it, as it were, just to the south here—the locals still-talked of that soon-day when the railroad would come to town.

But back to our huntsman:

It was along these tracks—that is the railroad's rails, running past the south of the town—that our huntsman rode out; here also alongside the Touchet River—which the locals called the 'Too-she' on account of most of them not speaking the French it was named in.

And the Touchet was a modest waterway; too wide to cross only in spots, but to where it did water trees and underbrush enough to offer, if need be, concealment, here and there, for both a man *and* his horse.

But as the river and the rails parted their ways, to the east of the town, our huntsman soon-decided to follow the railway's narrow maintenance path that ran beside the tracks, as that path was at-present in a better condition than the more-frequented Dayton Road— which in its Mullan capacity was still serving as an occasional road for military movements and so was prone to be still-soggy this deep into winter, and so still-deep in ruts, and so still-best to be avoided if possible.

So this shoulder-path alongside the rails is what the hunter followed the rest of the morn and then on into the after-noon until finally he came upon the Pepper creek.

And he crossed the Pepper creek at a little pooling spot beneath a fresh-built trestle which still reeked of creosote, and got off and watered his horse and took some quick lunch in an egg he'd purchased off Miss Norma and some crackers he got at the grocery.

Then he rode not north, up the Pepper Creek ravine, but due *northeast* at an angle instead, to get the lay of the slope on that gentle hill and to find a sneakier path that'd lead him up to his bounty, and to stake out a spot for the night to camp, and to watch.

He didn't suppose he'd run across Constance here anyhow, or if he did he'd be surprised, so as he rode he took to verse a little, for the horse:

"I grew up tall as the Indian corn," he sang, *"my pop had jist bits ta lend me, but'e give me'is great ol powderhorn, an'is woodsman's skills ta friend me."*

"With a leather shirt up-on my back an a redskin noose unravel," and he patted his beast on its neck, *"each forest sign I did carry my pack, so far as a scout could travel."*

And then he paused for a moment and looked out over the soft grey-sky hills of the Prescott valley, covered in knee-high grass of a buckskin hue, left from over the winter. And he stopped his horse a moment and he just listened to the eerie howl the wind was making as it blew through the stalks.

"What'dya reckon boy?" he asked all-of-a-sudden. Then he got his animal walking again as he was not-yet satisfied he'd found a suitable spot to keep an eye out.

"Til I lost my boyhood an found a wife," he started

again, *"a girl like a Salem clipper; a broad as straight as a huntin knife, with eyes bright as the Dipper."*

And here he turned and looked back, to check behind him. And the view here was too clear so he'd be seen were the boy to head down anywhere near the creek. So he kept on walking though they both, man and beast, were wore down from two-day's travel.

"Next comes my favorite part:" he finally told the horse,

"We cleared our camp where the bu'flo'd feed, upheards-of streams our flagons, an I sowed my sons like the apple-seed, ha! On the trail a the Western wagons!"

Then a deer up ahead caught his eye.

"They was right, tight boys, never sulky r slow. A fruitful an goodly muster."

And the deer's ears were on him, but it did not yet move.

"The eldest died at the Alamo. The youngest fell'th Custer."

Then the deer bolted.

And then, finally, burnt out, he decided he'd found his spot. He climbed down, tied-up his horse and started unpacking for camp.

He found his kindling quick and he didn't bother to walk across the hill, over to the brush, for fuel wood. There were thick-enough stalks for his purpose nearby. He broke a few, gathered up some handfuls of the thicker grass, cleared his spot, and made-up his fire. And by this time the sun was setting, and unpacked and generally settled, he just let his fire burn a minute and just watched as the sun slipped down the valley.

And he marveled upon the sky, thick with layer-upon-layer of colorful cloud.

And he marveled on the stories he'd heard, of how thisall is supposed to be the round ball of a planet twirling in blank space, supposed to be curved down but to where you clung to it no matter whichway it curves.

He never could grasp it fully, but that never did stop him from marveling on it the same.

"I miss the golden sunsets so," he started, singing again, though not in any particular key, *"the radiance a the dying day. I miss the tender rosy glow, as the last sunbeams die away.*

"I miss the sun's last parting smile, as rolling down the west.

"And gazing calm, down the while, hind the hills he sinks ta rest."

And the moon rose slow too, behind him as he cooked his beans, so the night stayed bright and he could see the lay of the land and, he thought, would see a shadowy figure were he to be approached.

And the beans were fine.

He thought of making some coffee too but decided against it.

And then, late-enough, he decided to turn in. First, though, he checked his horse, double-checked the lead, where he'd staked it in, then patted his animal on its side.

"Don't worry son. Bear don't come down out the mountains all too often." And he looked around one last time. "Not like cougar," he said, then stamped out his fire.

"You keep an eye out for'em wouldya?"

He laid on the ground, on his one blanket, wrapped the other over him, thought to wind his watch before the night, then rolled his arm around until he found the proper spot for its use as a pillow. And then, finally, with not the chirp of a single bird nor the chitter of a single insect, he closed his eyes and listened to the chill air as it slid its way through the stems on the hill.

"I miss the golden sunsets," he whispered, "the radiance a the dyin day. I miss the tender rosy glow, as the sunbeams die away."

He yawned.

"I miss the sun's last partin smile, rollin slowly down the west. An gazin, calm, down the while, hind the hill,

"he sinks ta rest."

Was good to be back to work.

THIS GRAND OL'
AMERICAN DREAM

✣

He was quite relieved when the morn greeted him with a glowing sky but not-yet the sun peeking over the mountains. And when he dug for his timepiece he saw it was before six still. So he woke up slow, comforted by the breathing of his nearby horse, and by the still-lingering smell of last-night's fire. But thoughts of his work soon filled his mind and agitated him from his blankets, and anxious to get this overwith he rolled his bedding quick and skipped his coffee and his breakfast and was soon packed-up and atop his horse.

And it wasn't more than an hour before he was atop the bluff.

And right-off he found the homestead-to-be, about a half-mile down, closer to where Pepper Creek drops into the valley.

But even from his ways off he suspected the place was empty.

But he rode in regardless and he found the camp and rode in close to survey it. And he found what there was to find of the building, which was only half-built. And he rode closer still and soon he saw there was no fire and

53

only one horse in the pen.

He inspected the new construction and took the lay
of the land and saw how they'd arranged the homestead
to look out upon a sweeping view that would make any
heart sing.

And then a funny thought came to him: That no one
gets to be so happy. In fact, he thought, here's proof.
This boy, Constance, had taken aim and swung for it,
so-to-speak, and instead hit his father-in-law-to-be in the
back, so-to-speak, and now he'd inherit none of this and
would never homestead here and would not settle upon it
a family.

Now had anyone thought to ask Isaac *his* thoughts
beforehand, while this deal was just in the arranging
phase, of what would come of this young couple; if
they'd live a long life, raise up their kids together on this
plot and age together and someday be buried under these
sparse trees, he'd a said no.

No way. No how.

Least not by what he'd ever seen.

The huntsman had heard his whole life all-about this
grand ol American dream; from this-or-that person, or in
this-song-or-that, or from some late-night spoutings in
the back corners of this dive or that. He was even guilty
of it himself to a certain degree, in his own sometimes-
after-sex conversings—especially with a particularly
beautiful ho he used to see regular there a bit.

And he'd met those unfortunate-enough to act on
such dreams. His brother for one, when he married,
and when Isaac had paid visit to their plot out in the
Willamette; and then gotten the letter first that their

boy'd died, then that their next-born come-out dead, and then that she'd died—and that was the last he ever heard, on his brother or his dreams.

And he'd often wondered on that.

He'd often wondered what his own parents had dreamt up in moving their clan out West; fore Mom got sick an fore Dad took solace in drinkin, then the gun.

But Isaac listened to what it is nature's always preaching, about the fate of the dreamers and their daring to hope for more than the scant bits she'd offer up on her own; so if anyone'd asked he'd a told em: these-here folk plain asked too much, to live out here where it's so beautiful. Which was a shame cause it was *a spot o' land* and woulda made a dream come true; were it not for the fate of reality seeing to it that dreams should *always* wilt-up, fore they ever really have chance to grow.

The farmhouse, or what-of-it there was, was sturdy. The half was covered with roofing to make convenient shelter, and here Constance had been recently, as there was dirt thrown over the fire fresh and this-close it still smelt of smoke.

Out in the pen a grey horse seemed happy eating at grass and didn't appear none desperate for water, and the view from right-up-near the house was especially nice with trees framing a picture of bluffs that rolled off into the hills then up into the Blue Mountains. Was almost the place for a church, were it not for the hike up-to it.

And then under one of those trees doing the framing he saw a curious pile of rocks and realized, quick, it was stones piled up over Mister Piedmont.

He waited there awhile.

Though he did not expect Constance to show.

He pailed some water for his horse, from the pump beside the fence.

He looked over the framing of the house somemore, to find where Constance might've hid weapons.

He didn't find any.

He checked behind the trees for any devices might be used against him.
And then, satisfied, he rode out back to town cause despite the Sheriff's prediction, Constance Lowrey wasn't home.

THE
STORY OF
OL' IRON

The Prescott valley was, as was mentioned previously, until recently not called the Prescott Valley atall, but was *presently* called the Prescott valley even in stories from before for the simple reason that it lacked a prior name.

Now it has been speculated by geologists that the valley, and in fact perhaps the entirety of the greater Palouse, was created during some catastrophic event; where once-upon-some-time a huge rush of water must have come washing through and created the soft hills and cut though them here in the valley all-of-a-sudden rather than over some prolonged period—may-be it was the great flood itself—and all this to say that today, despite the softness of the rolling hills, the bluffs either-side-of the Prescott valley, though they looked kind and gentle, could go steep on you all-of-a-sudden.

And here the sides were deceptively at that steep incline so that one minute you might think you're going gentle down a hill and then, if you lost attention, the hill'd go sideways on you without so much as a warning and you'd find yourself, in the best case, off your horse and on your post·er·iere, and in a worst case on the ground with your horse ontopaya.

Now Isaac knew this from the previous time when he'd rode through this very land, on this side even, to see over the valley for his bounty's trail. And it was of interest to him now to think on how even though the land was near-unchanged, how much different *he* was from that younger version of himself. Back then he was full of ideas. Back then it was fun, even, to think he could kill a man and get-away with it. But back then he didn't understand quite his place in the order of things. Not like he did now. Back then he didn't care so much about stuffs like the due process of law as looking a bad man in the eye and feeling the thrill—and not even the slightest guilt—at putting a bullet through the man's chest. Back then the chase, and the hunt, was the thrill. But over time it had started to wear as the good Lord saw fit to challenge him; such as that time he met the woman—by the first name Sally as he recalled, though he could no longer remember her last. She'd turned gun on him in an ambush just outside her husband's property when Isaac came round to inquire as to the why and how of her man shot dead.

That was a blast-through-the-face he did not thrill upon, either at that time or after.

Didn't feel right to shoot a woman.

Still don't.

And then there was the kid.

"I ever tell you bout Ol Iron?" the huntsman said, so sudden a tremor ran down the side of his horse.

"Didn't mean ta startle ya," he said, "Just got ta thinkin, I otta fill ya in on yer predecessor."

And the horse kept one ear on him as he spoke.

"Ol Iron was-a-beast; only way ta put it. Sixteen-han-an-three, dark grey wit some red to it, kinda like the metal s where'e got the name. A beau·ty cept'e kept puttin'imself through fences, had scars all up an down'is undersides."

And Isaac scanned the valley still and could see nearly to the town that the road was clear.

"Had'im, oh, bout six years, til this green blacksmith down La Grande way shoed'im wrong an'e threw'is leg out. Got'im when'e's… six, as I recall, so this's at… twelve I'spose.

"Still young, so I ended up turnin'im loose."

They rode on a little while.

"I did not have heart ta shoot that horse, even with'is no-good leg."

"I imagine he is dead by-now."

"Anyways, Iron an I got ta be pretty good company. Kinda like you an I are startin ta be…

"Now *there's* a horse knew'is master."

"An you'll learn too, I imagine. But… I'd get quiet an he'd get quiet. I'd get loud an he'd get loud too."

"Sure do miss'im sometime."

And then as if it knew what it was his master was saying, the beast snorted something fierce, and this further fueled Isaac's long-harbored suspicion that over time even a horse would learn to pick up bits of the human language.

"Oh don't worry son," he called and patted the horse against its neck, "You're a fine one. I ain't lookin ta replace ya."

And Isaac stood up tall in the saddle to keep an eye over the ridge, anxious to find any hint of Constance and to oversee the dispensing of justice.

But so far nothing.

"Years back," he finally kept on, "old Iron saved me from quite a bit a trouble.

"I get called-up ta this sorta… hamlet, up in the Blues, not far from the Toll Gate. An this ain't yer typical gangster hideaway story er the man-fraid-a-justice. This one's a boy. Like a baby boy. Well…" he stammered: "seven, or maybe it's eight as memory serves; thought to've killed'is own mother then turn'n run. Story's in the papers an at-that-time there's still some confusion as ta which's Oregon territory and what's Washington an exactly where the border belongs, an anyhow my bondsman-at-that-time passed me a telegram sayin the Sheriffs'd had enough an could *I* please track the boy an bring'im in fer due process, jist ta get the matter resolved. Which's all fine an good only they failed ta inform me *the boy's de-ranged*!" he laughed, "which's the kinda thing a bounty man needs ta know wouldn'tcha say?"

"Anyhow, hunt starts easy-nuff. Talked with the father. He's outta sorts, as you'd spect, losin'is wife to'is kid. He's the one told me the boy's de-ranged. Anyhow, we's trackin'im, Iron an I. An this's maybe early Nov·ember so it's cold, specially up in those mountains, so I'm part concerned the boy'll freeze. An in cases such anyhow you don't know *what* ta think on the de-ranged, specially up in the woods when they got ta be round firearms day-ta-day? So parta me kinda feels sorry for'im.

"Anyhow, we's track'n'im. An first day I'm kinda-mazed how much groun this kid's coverin.

"Second day same deal. Some'nlike forty mile a night this boy's makin, so you could tell'e's near-runnin throughout; an now you tell me, what kinda eight-year-old you ever hearda could make that kinda pace? I almost thought I's on the wrong trail. But then, third day, we catch up to'im. An now this's forest country so it ain't like we'da jist walked up on'im. But by now Iron got the jist a what it is we did—an this's what I miss bout'im so—come that third morn we smelt a fire. An I know we's waay deep in the woods ta be on a cabin so we know we got'im. An so Iron..." and the huntsman could not help but smile, "...sneaked up on'im, real quiet. Quieter'n you'd think a horse could sneak. An as we're ta where we can see the smoke I get off. An I tell Iron ta wait. An that horse's such a steed! *I did not even have ta tie him up!*"

"Unlike you."
"But that's alright."

"You'll get there."

"Anyhow, I'm sneakin through the unerbrush an...

jist as I'm gittin ta where I can see'im, an as I come up-on'im, I realize… the boy's sleepin. Jis passed out there on the groun. He'd made'im a fire an jist plain fell ta sleep! Which's no wonder since the boy'd pushed clean through three nights in a row. But this's where they'll gitcha. Cause I ain't never had ta deal with no de-ranged eight-year-old before, an from the look of'im the boy's… well… he jist looked a boy. Sweet ya might call it an… well, more-r-less a sleepin babe. An ya hear things bout the de-ranged; how their heads ain't on straight, but it's another thing entire ta come cross such malady in the person.

"Anyhow I don't know much bout allthis yet so sufferin a moment a softness, I suppose, I sneaked in on'im real close, an…" and here the hunter shook his head, "insteada wakin'im with my barrel to'is face, like I otta… I jist… kinda… tapped'im, on the shoulder. An stupid me, I say, jist like this, all soft an sweet an gentle I say, 'wake up son. Wake up. Come on. Come on kid. Let's get ya warm'n fed.'

"An ya know what that boy did? He pulls a revolver out'is jacket an'e say'd mister, I'm'a shootja! So I said, why you wanna do a thing like that!?!

"But the boy…" and Isaac shook his head again.

"'is eyes. They's cold. Like I seen in the worsta'em. The *very* worst. The one's ain't know better. An here's that spirit, alive in this tiny… jist, sweet little boy."

"Anyhow, it's pretty clear right then-n-there the boy had me. Had gun-to-my-face an wasn't interested in negotiatin neither. An I thought sure I's dead an I thought I'd never hear the en of it. …ta be killed by a child… But ya know what? Iron, that ol horse! I do not know what got in to'im, besides bein jist-bout the best horse there ever could be, but allofasudden Iron lept out those trees an charged right for the boy! An insteada shootin at me the boy shot him, n got'im, right in the shoulder."

"Never did get that bullet out."
Then Isaac shut his mouth.

And it was awhile, until they were near down the ridge, before he spoke again.

"I did not have much time ta think on it. Kindajust… reacted ya know.
"Anyhow, shot the boy in the chest right back, pretty high up. Caught'is lung. An he's there coughin an sputterin. An I say to'im, 'what'd ya think's gonna happen kid?' An'e gist's screamin: Ima killya! Ima killya! An I tell'im, cause I ain't sure how many rounds he got left, I tell'im, 'calm down son. Calm down. You know that you have shot your own momma? Ain't that right? Do you know that ain't normal?' An the kid's cryin; but it's kinda hard ta tell if it's from sadness r jist from the pain a bein shot. But then the kid catches me by surprise, cause he don't ask bout'is momma atall. Ya know, cause I wasn't sure'e knowed she's dead. An I kinda thought mention of-it might tone'im down some. But'e don't seem phased by her dead atall."
The hunter shook his head.
"He jist asked bout'is pop. But'e asked, 'did I get Papa too?' An I told'im, no, yer papa's fine. An ya know, *the kid shouts an explicative*! I won't even repeat it to ya; but I still cain't believe. To this day! The boy's upset

he *only* killed'is momma, not both!"

And here they came to the road and Isaac guided his horse alongside the railroad tracks, as they ran next to the main trail here.

And he scanned the hills.

And he saw not a soul.

"Anyhow, turned out the boy'd jist the one bullet remainin—an I'm hind a tree fer the bulk a the rest a this—an Iron's jist planted tween me an the boy; an we's shoutin all this across'im… Anyhow, he clicked'is trigger an once I hear there's no bullets I jist walked over an whalloped'im cross the back of'is head. Bandaged'im up best I could an by the time I'd rode'im round to'is pop I had a dispatch waitin for me from the local Justice, sayin ta leave the boy with'is father, ta dispense *parental* justice."

"Still don't know if I agree."

"Was a tough one."

And just then Isaac saw a figure emerge from around the bend up ahead and he felt himself straighten up fast.

"Any how," he hushed to the animal, "you can see why I couldn't shoot that horse, even if it's the humane thing. By that point I'd jist had enough a shootin, when it come ta him anyhow."

Now Isaac's eyes were good in the distance, even from atop a horse, but the sun was right over his head by this time, to where he had some trouble sizing the traveler up. But he did reckon right-off it was a man, or a boy at least, wearing a hat and a heavy jacket, which was about right for the cold of the day.

And the fellow rode with confidence and at the least
did not seem concerned to come across a stranger on the
road.

And telling, the man appeared to have both his arms.

When he was finally close enough Isaac drew in
a deep breath then bellowed out, loud, "HALLOW,
FRIEND!"

"Howdy yourself," came the shout back. And the
voice was a young one but plenty cheery and not-at-all
in distress or conflicted.

"SAY" Isaac shouted again, "MIND IF I ASK YER
NAME?"

"Name's Farlow. Terrence. You?"

"LAPLACE. ISAAC LAPLACE."

And by-now they were close-enough they could
see each other's faces, and Isaac's suspicion did grow.
The boy was young, but maybe too young. Looked to
be mid-teen; with clear skin and maybe more brown
hair than sandy. He did not match the drawing but that
was not entirely uncommon; so the best clue was that
arm, except for how cold the day was and how stiff the
jacket and for the boy having gloved hands so that if this
boy was not Terrence Farlow but was in-fact Constance
Lowrey only pretending to be, and so did have just his
one arm, it was not immediately clear.

"Passing through from Dayton?" the boy's voice
came from the distance.

"NO. UP, FROM THE COUNTY SEAT."

But the while Isaac was busy thinking on a way to
ask the boy to raise up his arms.

But he knew, also, the bountyman's warrant,
while it extends upon the land of the hunted, does *not*

extend onto public property, nor any other *besides* the hunted's—except for special circumstances—and that were he not careful such questioning could leave him vulnerable to accusations of unlawful search.

"How'd you come in?" the boy asked, "The Hart road or the lower Waitsburg?"

"HART. SAY, I'M LOOKIN FOR CONSTANCE LOWREY. YOU SEEN'IM?"

"Sure, sir. He's up with Mr. Piedmont, up at the Piedmont plot; back the way you came, up on your north, just past Pepper Creek."

"YOU SEEN'IM?"

"Just last week."

"NOT SINCE THEN?"

"No, sir."

"HOW DO YA KNOW HE'S THERE?"

"Everyone knows that mister. He's up there homesteadin fore he marries ol Piedmont's daughter Narcissa."

Isaac nodded.

"What'd you say yer name was agin?" he asked the boy, close enough now to talk.

"Terry Farlow. I'm farm hand for the Lamperts."

Isaac nodded.

"And you, sir? What'd you say was yours?"

"Isaac LaPlace."

THE
IDENTIFICATION
OF
CONSTANCE LOWREY

Having skipped his breakfast to examine the
Piedmont plot, and having loitered there awhile, and
then having taken his time to return back to Prescott as
well, the huntsman was quite starving by the time he got
back to the town proper and near-falled back into the
Pleasant Pheasant when he did arrive; for a cooked meal
and for the soft, if slight, company of Miss Norma, and
for just a quiet place to sit awhile.

But being this mid into the afternoon Miss Hatcherly
appeared to be closing up her shop.

But as he'd tipped very well earlier and tried to
remain so pleasant, she did seem glad to meet him again
and agreed to cook him some potatoes and corn and
some canned tomatoes she still had on-hand, and to offer
him the same issue of the *Walla Walla Statesman*, which
he kindly refused but thanked her the same.

Rather he thought he'd just sit awhile and stew maybe, as his recent encounter on the road was still fresh on his mind, and the difficulty of his position, of needing to identify a boy from nothing more than a wanted flyer; and the fact he couldn't ask no one for help neither, til he'd already rode the boy down to the jailhouse.

Now if this boy was smart, enough to go unidentified, give false name or to otherwise evade, he could make life real difficult for a huntsman, so Isaac set his mind to thinking on ways he could trap Constance into showing his one arm, or at the least into a lie would grant warrant to search his person and expose that one identifying arm, or lack thereof, the same. But the fear—which's the same fear he always got when on the job—was that he'd short-cut his way into a mistake and he'd hear about it from the bonds company; or if he took too long too, if he declared too many expenses, or if he even just plain give-up.

But worse—and he'd thanked the good Lord this never had happened—at least not yet anyhow—but worse was the chance of killing a by-stander, especially over a matter of mis-identification.

Not that he'd lose his post. The law expected that from time to time a man may be killed on accident. In fact in this respect his position was something of the soldier's where unless he *meant* to kill, *im*proper, or intentional in-other-words, he was to be excused the occasional slip.

He feared more on how it would weigh on him. Not that by-now it'd give him a shock or break him down. Nothing like that. More, that to keep from sticking on it the way some of his stories did already he'd have to clam up and get colder inside, and he was cold enough inside already.

"Here's your tatoes mister," Norma announced then gently set a plate down before him.
"Much obliged," Isaac responded, and Miss Norma did a little curtsy and he noticed her face was a little red, for it was just the two of them in there now. So he was careful not to give sign of interest, for she was less than half of his age.
Rather he just ate his grub and just stewed.

"So, whatcha doin back in town so soon?" Miss Hatcherly dared ask. And this caught Isaac once-again off-his-guard, so it took him a bite to reply:

"Workin miss. I'm on a job. I, uh, had appointment with Mr. Hector Piedmont. Rode up to'is place but no one's home."
"Huh," she replied. "That's queer. Cause ya jist missed'is son-in-law."
"Constance?"
"Yep. Stopped by maybe a hour ago?"

"Never seen the boy but I'm familiar with'im. What's he look like?"
"Oh, I never know how to describe no one. Got medium-length hair, smooth face, no beard. Kinda big ears? He's a tall boy; looks younger'n'e is, which's good cause Narcissa looks so young too, fer her age. Uh, you know he's missin the arm."
"Yalp."
"Kay. Well otherwise jist, kinda normal boy."

"You know a Terrence Farlow?"

"Sure. I know Terry. Out at Lampert's."

"What's *he* look like?"

"Huh. Not like Constance. Tween you an me he's ugly. No other way ta put it. Gangly kid. Real skinny, long nose, an teeth stick out from'is face."

"Huh… You member what Constance's wearin?"

"Grey coat as I recall. Black hat. Brown horse."

"That so."

"To the best a my recollection mister."

"Huh."

The huntsman turned back to his plate and stewed somemore.

It was not often he was had.

But then he remembered he was having a conversation.

"I thank you, kindly. Better get eatin."

"Certainly mister."

THING TO UNDERSTAND 'BOUT THE BOUNTYMAN

✜

The thing to understand 'bout the bountyman, he considers himself distinct from the rest of everybody. And he's got to.

Unlike the common man, or even a proper officer-of-the-law, the bounty man lives outside the law distinctly. And yet unlike the soldier, who has a commander and the company of his fellows to fight alongside, the bountyman goes it alone.

Now yes a bounty killer has a bondsman as boss and solicitor and more-often-than-not a Deputy or the Sheriff or a district Judge beside, but the mandate that bonds the bounty hunter, especially as used in these territories, was as a last-case, for when all the usual tools of the law did not-quite fit the bill.

And yes in the common instance the function of the bountyman is clear as day. When a crime is committed

the law will see fit to set a hearing and then will oft turn
the accused out on a bail in which a monetary stake is
intended to assure the return of the person to the court at
the time of hearing. And all the bountyhunter is supposed
to be for is to go out, hunt-down, and collect-up such
waywards who have skipped out on their appearance;
come hell or high water, out-side what the commoner
might see as the law just as well as in it, sometimes dead
just as well as alive, and for a good fee too.

But of late the local governments had begun
imagining a new use for the position the bounty killer
occupied, and the unique absolution his post is afforded;
that of the rogue—in a very narrow sense of the word; of
a man acting alone, with-out the common law explicitly,
as it were, though still with intent to protect it.

Now in the case you heard before, where Isaac
was telling his horse about the deranged child he near-
killed, such was a case where, rather than argue as to
jurisdiction, the Sheriffs of the competing Counties
sought the employ of a bountyman as a 'neither-nor'
scenario in which the allegiance of the bounty hunter
could be assured beyond geographics. Otherwise it'd just
been a job for the local department.

But as Isaac found himself more-and-more in
conversation with law men grown-frustrated with the
trappings and limitations upon the law he did notice a
general slipping of these men-of-government into what
he recognized might-well wind up murky-and-dangerous
waters.

Now this business today, between the elder
Piedmont and the young master Lowrey, was not the
case yet. Isaac understood that Constance Lowrey was a
delicate example and that were this still-fledgling town

to focus on this-side-or-that of the dealings regarding Hector's death instead of on keeping to the business of sowing their land and nursing their stock, they could-well fall, inadvertent, into a state where the normal sharings and cooperations necessary to the farmer could grow impossible, and to where the town couldwell fail.

But already he could see it in the eyes of these Sheriffs, lost in their own mandates so far as to forget their job is to uphold the rule of law and to see where the rule of those laws gets, and not to see justice done in their own eyes by whatever means they might deem necessary. Such justice was, he'd heard told—back in his schooling and in some of his more intelligenced conversings—the justice of the *old* Sheriffs, who were landlords more, over their own serfs, before a free land was established, and before the expectation was fortified that all men should be held as equals, under identical rules, and to the same consequence.

So in this way Isaac saw himself as what he hoped was a dying breed. Still, yes, there were difficulties in building up a free nation, and yes those difficulties did justify, for the time being, the rare operator who should break rules for the sake of the rules (or the rule, as it were) of a Republic; over the heads, so to speak, of those who would break the rules for their own causes—'cause exploitation in the name of self-interest is not how one behaves insuch. But as he'd, over these years, become more familiar with the bountyman's position he was, more-and-more, caught up in a growing conflict within himself; between his hope that the bountyman would be needed less-and-less and a realization that rather it was becoming quite the opposite, to where the lawman was slipping more-and-more into the old ways; to where he was recoursing more-and-more to the bountyman's *lawlessness.*

But regardless he had to stop these thoughts as he'd come out of Prescott fast on his horse, after his lunch, to a fork in the road where before him continued his way back to Pepper Creek and on up to the Piedmont Plot beyond, but to his right was the Hart road, up to Piedmont's Homestead:

"Now," he finally said, aloud in the company of his horse, his voice disturbing the silence beneath the gentle breeze "if I'm Constance I got a choice ta make here, don't I?"

And his horse turned one ear.

"So I assume he ain't skippin town. Least that's not the sense I got from'im this morn. He wasn't packed ta run. So, assumin he come back inta town ta resupply, his scenario here's, he could keep on straight an go back up an wait ta defend'imself; *or,* havin met'is hunter an knowin I'm on'is trail, he *could* slip up there ta the Homestead of'is beloved an see'is bride one last time fore settlin in near'is evidence fer whatever it is this kid has in mind ta do bout our confrontation."

The horse waited.

"Not much of a choice, is it?"

And were it Old Iron he would have expected the beast to snort. But this one was another type and just stood his ground and just waited to be told what to do.

NANCY & NARCISSA

✝

Having rode hard out of Prescott after his meal, and after tipping Miss Norma well again, and even after getting to the fork in the road quick and making his decision to aim his pursuit up the hill and toward the Piedmont Homestead, Isaac was now quite pleased with how his horse had crossed the Touchet and how it had taken its water quick and how it wasn't too anxious for grass despite the cold.

But the Hart road turned steep not long out of the valley and soon the beast was working plenty and its sides were bellowing fury so that even though the sun was sinking quick Isaac did think to ease up on the animal, as there was still much work left and they'd be a ways from the waters of the river for some time. So he trotted the animal, and as he went he got to figuring on how it was he should approach Missus Piedmont; on account of knowing her husband was dead, and on account of having some humane responsibility to her, but also responsibility to his position not to offer any information might cause her to interfere.

At first he thought he might suggest, mysterious

though it would be, that she check in on her husband
maybe in a few days time. But this he dismissed quick.
It would be too odd and would surely tip her off as to
a problem, or could bring about questioning as to his
meaning which could reveal more than he intended.

He considered playing the part of a regular sport
hunter inquiring upon having a hunt on the Piedmont
property. But the season was off and anyhow it wouldn't
give him much information as Missus Piedmont could
herself give him a yes or a no; and anyway it would raise
suspicion if he were to ask for the Master of the property
instead of her. This was America afterall and even a
woman has certain rights when it comes to her husband's
land.

So finally, just as he reached the top of the hill, and
just as he could see the Piedmont house off in the far
distance, out over the green oat, he decided it would be
best just to ask as to Mister Piedmont plain, that way if
the women were to raise any question he could hint that
it's a matter best kept secret and they'd have to assume
the matter regarded some bridal arrangement; such that
Missus Piedmont might simply tell him what he asked
and avoid further discussion in front of the bride-to-be,
so-as not to spoil a surprise.

So as he turned from the main road, and as he
slowed his horse down somemore, and as he walked
their lane, and as his horse was still puffing from being
rode so hard, he thought to get off his mount and to
approach the property on foot so the coming of a
stranger this close to dark would not cause undue worry
upon the two gentler souls.

And as he finally approached the house proper he
was careful to keep eye out for any sign of Constance,

for even in the failing light he could see fresh hoof prints.

But he could see candles burning in the kitchen and could discern a body in that window, who finally looked up and saw him and then made for the front door:

"Hello!" Isaac called when he saw Missus Piedmont emerge.

"How do you do?" she called from her distance.

"Fine, ma'am. An I apologize for the late hour."

And to this she stood her ground well and it was clear she was practiced at handling these calls and wasn't much afraid.

"It's fine," she called out. "In fact we have supper on, if you're in need of any."

"No, ma'am. I thank you. I am wondering, mostly, if I am in the right place. You Missus Piedmont?"

"Yes."

"Oh good."

Then Narcissa came out on the porch too, beside her mother.

"That must make you Narcissa."

"That's right," the young girl offered.

And then her Mother nudged her.

"Yessir."

And the Sheriff was right. She was fresh as a blossom, with milky skin and already-carved cheek bones, and rich hair and a straight upright back and a refinement that genuinely disturbed the huntsman's train of thoughts.

"Well…" Isaac finally continued, "I'm mostly wonderin if I might speak at *Mister* Piedmont a moment.”

“Mister Piedmont is away,” Missus Piedmont gave up, though sternly, “Might I convey a message? Or would you rather go to him direct?”

But Isaac watched Narcissa rather, for any slight hesitance; any bit of wary in her eyes; a glance cast toward the barn or down the road, or for her listening for the back door so she might know Constance was safely away. But this was not what Isaac saw but instead a direct engagement and a genuine curiosity, and maybe even a smile upon her lips that matters concerning Mister Piedmont, by this stage, were matters concerning her wedding and her bright, expectant future; so that Isaac knew these two did not presently harbor Constance and that neither had Constance warned them of the events which had transpired.

“I think I would rather go to him direct, if it’s possible.”

“It is,” Missus Piedmont nodded, “He’s over across the valley, most of a day’s ride,” and she pointed off in the general direction of the anticipated homestead.

“Well,” she corrected, “it’s about three hours.”

“Again I thank you, an I do appreciate it. Can you give me direction?”

“You know the Pepper Creek?”

“I do,” he said. He did not want the whole run-down.

“Well, you turn north just past it. Head up the bluff and you won’t miss it. Just look for some scattered pines.”

“Got it.”

“You can stay the night, if you need, but probably in the barn.”

"Ma'am I am much obliged, but the moon is plenty bright an I can camp down in the valley."

"Suit yourself. Narcissa, you better check that pot."

"Yes ma'am."

And Narcissa turned inside.

And Isaac waited.

And Missus Piedmont seemed none surprised by his hesitation.

"Missus Piedmont?" the hunter finally asked, "My visit concerns some arrangements regardin the weddin."

"I thought it might."

"By chance, is the young Lowrey with Mister Piedmont?"

"I expect so by now."

"By now?"

"Well he was just back here this afternoon to fetch some stuffs. If you'd been a couple hours earlier he could've escorted you."

"Oh," Isaac said. "An ya say go down ta the Valley an meet the Dayton road, til I come ta the Pepper Creek."

"Yes."

"Know if there's a cross-road?"

"I'm afraid not, without crossing plowed field."

"Huh," Isaac said. "Curious. So I come up outta Prescott, *up* Hart road, an I did not passim on my way here."

"You came from town?"

"Through the town."

"About what time?"

"Oh, I musta set off mid-afternoon, after I'd had some lunch."

"That *is* strange."

Missus Piedmont did seem genuinely perplexed.

"He might've been fishing, along the creek, when you passed," she offered. And while it hardly satisfied the huntsman, Isaac was sure to act like it did.

"That musta been it. Well, ma'am, agin I thank ya."

"Alright sir. Safe travels."

"You have a good eve."

" THAT SEEM
A BIT ODD
TA YOU?   "

Before he leaved Missus Piedmont did kindly offer Isaac the trough to water his horse, and he did oblige before heading out; and then waved in return to their waving-off as he left, just at dusk. But the while he kept himself focused on Constance, in part so-as not to trouble so much on the sadness was about to descend upon that household.

May be, he thought, when all's said-and-done the community might come together and support these two ladies and help maintain their home, even if they'd likely lose their stead—and almost certainly lose the plot. Of course he knew their chance was slim. Life here was hard and such property would not stand to sit long fore someone would offer them up a deal would force their move, probably to nearer civilization, where Missus Piedmont would become a widow—*may be* with a purse to last her—and Narcissa would surely find her way onto the arm of some lucky-enough bachelor, and that would be that.

But back to Constance; Isaac did not know whether to thank or to curse the moon. On the one hand the brightness of the night meant that if Constance were around, still, to keep track of his hunter, or to lay ambush, the moon would certainly help the boy see what's going on and help him accomplish his means to that end. After-all Constance would certainly be more inclined to stick round in the brightness instead of rushing back to beat the dark. But on the other it meant that if Constance *were* up to something, that moon would make it harder for the boy to get the jump.

As it were anyhow the huntsman could see the road up ahead just fine, and the Valley that stretched out below, down to the fields, and to the trees that lined the river.

"I tell ya," he said to his horse, "this Constance's a slippery fella."

And this time the horse did snort a little and it surprised Isaac.

"Thing bout one-arms... their one arm's got ta do the work a two," he said, "so theys strong."

It wasn't that he felt outmatched. By no means. He could take a teener without strain, less one with half the arms. It's more, he knew that if there's one thing to respect in this world it's what a challenge'll do for a man.

"We'll stop soon ol boy," he said and patted the

beast on its neck, "when we get down ta the river."

And they kept on walking with his kit clanking and the horse's shoes clacking and no other sound to speak of to mask it.

"They say they mind has ta work harder too," he added, "learnin how ta do things with half the arms, so they's smart alotta the time."

And the horse snorted again.

"Only thing the one arm *don't* tell me bout'im's'is intention."

And Isaac pondered on this awhile.

The boy certainly was the actor; when he'd claimed to be the farmhand, like he'd thought up the story already and maybe even rehearsed it some.

"He definitely give us the slip, that's fer sure," Isaac finally said. "Question is, why'd he do that?"

"Huh son? Ya got any ideas?"

But the horse did not snort this time.

"Why'd'e tell us who'e whudn't back there?"

"How'd'e *know* ta do that? That's a question. How'd he know a bountyman's after'im an not a uniform from the Sheriff's office?"

And they walked a little while this way, with Isaac's head swirling.

"This one's definitely smart."

"Smart nuff ta know what the Sheriff's thinkin."

"That seem a bit odd ta you?"

MOONLIGHT
DOWN THE VALLEY

✛

To hear it told the Prescott Valley could be a strange place after dark. Once the sun disappeared behind the hills and it was just purple left in the sky, a full moon would shine right down between those hills and make the same dark night-time shadows as the sun in the morn.

And it was in this light, of that big ol' moon, Isaac decided he didn't particularly like the look of the trees down near the river, with the waters running right through their middle and the loud babbling could hide the sound of footsteps in the brush. And he knew his horse wouldn't neither because the beast had its ears on those trees too and was fixing to throw a fuss and was getting snorty already:

"I hear ya bub. I hear ya," he assured the creature. "I don't like the look of em neither. N fact were I a bear you know where I'd hide?

"That's right. Right there in those tree."

So, close enough, he whoa'd his steed and decided, looking around, that his spot right there was fine as any, and if Constance meant him harm anyhow Isaac had a feeling he'd a tried by now. And if the boy wanted to hide to see by the light of that moon... well, there was no point in stoppin him neither.

"It's alright," he whispered as he began to bed them down, "It's alright. If you're good on water I'll jist graze ya here an we'll cross tomorra."

THE
DEAD
PART

✟

The next morn, despite his intention, Isaac woke upright to the sun shining on his face already, well above the mountains.

And were he Constance, the hunter reckoned, at this moment he'd certainly be watching this huntsman to size up what a boy could of the bountyman's intentions. So Isaac did his best to rise graceful and to seem together, even as he realized that this late past sunrise the boy could've already seen enough to make an impression. A wrong impression may-be; but that hardly mattered, as no impression could shield the boy from the draw of the hunter's bounty.

So the huntsman did not feel much the need to rush just yet. He reckoned today's the day anyhow and in his experience preparation gives the upper hand, so he packed his camp up calm-and-careful, cooked himself a tin of beans and undid his parcel of jerky and had a bite of that too.

"This boy's gonna do one a two things," he finally
spake to his horse, which was grazing nearby, and who
did not seem too anxious yet for water anyhow, "you jist
watch. He's either gonna run, if'e's smart, so far we'll
never find'im. …cause we ain't givin chase long. Not
for no three-hunred dollar. Or'e's gonna dig in'is heels.
Cause if'e's gonna throw'imself down ta the law he'd a
done it by now."

"He'd a done it back there on the road."
And Isaac scooped up the last bite of his beans, out
the tin with his finger, and then tossed the can on top the
chars of the fire. And then he stood up tall, stretched out,
and then gave his horse a good look-over.

"Yep boy, I have a feelin we might haffta work fer
our money taday.
"I jist hope the boy's smartnuff not ta wind up the
dead part."

A CAT,
AND A BIG ONE,
AND A MALE

✛

The hunter's eyes was wide.

He was hid, partial, in tall grass, up to near his shoulders, about halfway up the slope that lead up to the Piedmont bluff. And he was pleasantly surprised his horse was taking a hint and wasn't being so loud.

Now this getting on toward the early part of spring the songbirds were starting in on their business already, and were being good'n loud too. And there was a wind also, whipping across the grass, so Isaac knew he wouldn't be heard until he was damn-near on top someone. But regardless he kept his wide eyes to the horizon and led his horse by the rope, slow, on foot, up the slope.

To his right the hill rose up into underbrush but to his left was quite a ways before the hill turned down and ran into Pepper Creek ravine. And beyond the ravine he could see a couple far-off trees, up a ways and over on that side, and he took note that they'd make a good lookout were it not for his hunted being a one-arm, so not too likely to climb them.

Still he was not inclined to make *any* assumption; as so-doing was near-always what got the bountyman hurt, if not killed.

And soon he stopped at a pile of horseshit and he rolled it around with his boot to determine its age, and so-determined it to be less than a day old; which did alarm him some as he knew it was not from *his* horse and so strongly implied Constance likely *did* return over the night and so had the eve to prepare.

But of course the huntsman had met bigger challenges than some land-savvy teener who, though full of plenty of fresh strength, and no end to bright young ideals, and probably full of that excited desperation afforded by still-unfulfilled dreams of youth, alas lacked in the practical experience of try-and-failure and the proofs that come-from it, and the hardness comes from dreams killed in earnest by the nature of the world.

Nope. He knew he had the boy, even as he knew the boy thought otherwise.

And he kept on, his walking, and as he knew he was drawing nearer the plot he drew his horse in close so he could shoosh the thing at a sound.

And they crept on.

And soon they came to a level spot atop a small berm and were afforded something of a view of the slope above and how it lead up toward the homestead, and he looked around a moment to see if it was safe to come up on top of it. And it did look safe, or at the least he reckoned it'd be as hard for Constance to ambush him up there as for he to ambush Constance. So he stepped out, and he kept walking, on up the hill, and steeled himself so-as to be as ready as he could.

"Shhh…" he'd whisper to the horse, every so often.

"Shhh… It's okay."

"No need ta worry yerself. We're fine," he'd say.

"We's jist sneakin s'all. Nothin gonna git us. We's jist sneakin."

"Jist… be smart. N keep quiet."

"None-a this snortin business."

"I need ya ta keep settled."
Now Isaac knew it was nonsense to speak to a horse, as if the thing could understand a word he said. Yet he would speak in the company of his animals the same, for his theory, reticent though he was to admit it, that in truth a beast, of sufficient mindfulness, would come to understand, given time, if not the words themselves at the least some of the meanings behind them.

"We jist gotta be smart's all. This boy's worth keepin atopa."

Of course Isaac had been told that speech was what separates thinking man from the beasts of the field, and

as he recalled this was even in the Good Book itself,
where an ass took on speech by a miracle of the Lord.
Yet in his experience the more he talked the more a
creature would learn to listen, and even to talk back in its
own way.

"I ain't gettin shot fer no three hunred dollar. That's
fer damn sure."

If he hadn't seen it himself he never would have
believed it.
Of course the beast wouldn't respond with words,
but they would respond the way perhaps a mute child
might, in certain actions.

Though this was not his sole reason for speaking
aloud in the company of this horse of his, green as it
was, it was some part of it. How else, he reasoned,
would the horse learn the trade of being a huntsman's
steed if not from being told what was expected, in some
form or another.

It had certainly been the means of Ol' Iron's
enduring success. And bit by bit it was becoming the
case with this one too.

"Ya see those trees over there," he told, and pointed.
"We're gonna stay our distance, over here. Jist cause…
I don't think he's gonna, but if a man could, or a boy
could, it sure would be a spot-ta-be-hid, way up there,
wouldn't it? So we're jist gonna… stay over here, down
range, an not out there on top the ridge, cause then we'd

be waaay out in the open an ya'd see us from a mile."

And he kept leading his horse.

What was a man, afterall, Isaac thought as they made their way up the hill, but a creature himself. And Isaac had certainly seen men do darker things than even the worst of nature's predators. So, may be, he thought, there was more to the beasts of the Earth than they were given credit for.

He also spoke aloud because, though he was of some certainty that Constance was waiting for him up on the homestead-to-be, the boy may just as well be lying in the grass somewhere between here and there, so that were Isaac to sneak past in silence, there was some chance that the two might miss each other, and it was Isaac's preference to handle what the boy might attempt of an ambush then and there rather than prolong their confrontation any longer. Afterall he knew how to speak reason to a man, or a boy, so long as the parties kept their heads on straight. And if not, the huntsman knew what to do in that case too.

"Nah. We're gonna stick ta this right here. An I know ya ain't gonna like it, cause it kinda rises up overus a little, over here, but if he'd a hid up there we'd a seen'im from back down there a ways. So we're jist gonna follow this little rise in the slope, right here on up, til we git up on that *next* ridge. That way we--"

But the huntsman stopped dead and held exactly still 'cause his eyes, and he hoped not-yet those of his animal, had fallen upon a shape in the grass he recognized immediate to be that of a cat, and a big one, and a male.

He stepped back and reached slow for his rifle from his saddle but already it was too late. The horse pulled tense and then the damned horse bolted, tore the reins right from his hand and took his rifle along with it.

And of course this drew the cougar's attention and that thing tensed up too, turned to face Isaac, and spread its front legs wide in defense.

Now Isaac did turn to see what his chance was of bolting after his horse; but the thing was long gone, down the hill, and was stirring up a big cloud of dust behind it anyhow.

And already the cougar was crouching now toward Isaac. And it was here that the huntsman had such a moment he was always dread of, where his heart was pounding in his chest, and in his ears too, and his mouth went dry and the colors changed and he could hear, all-of-a-sudden, every noise in creation, and his thinking went real quick.

He checked his pockets but he knew his Colt wasn't yet loaded and his bullets were with the horse beside. He surveyed the ground for a rock but it was all this damn volcano powder and just little chunks of slab but nothing to throw. And his jacket was thick but he'd had occasion to see what the claws of such a cat could do, less the teeth. But still as the thing crouched low to leap for him he raised his arm beside and then in an instant he saw it in the air and then he saw it twist strange and blood tear out its chest and *then* he hear'd the shot. And in an other instant he knew what'd happened. He looked over to the trees and he saw a cloud of smoke and then the Cougar stumbled up from the ground beside him and turned and dashed off.

And Isaac gasped. And his vision went starry, but not so much he couldn't see a body jump from those trees and then a horse stampede up from the ravine and on up the hill.

"HEY!" he shouted after the boy, and gave chase; but he was winded and the boy's horse was off to a gallop with one-armed Constance on its back and then they were up over the hill and gone.

But Isaac near fell-over and was all-of-a-sudden so hot he threw off his outer jacket and he wheezed and he leaned over on his knees and, damned angry, he turned back down the hill and just watched as the cloud-a-dust that was all his belongings disappeared out of sight that way too.

"Damn!" he finally shouted.

And then he picked up his jacket, draped it over his arm, and got to walking.

LIGHTNIN' IN A BOTTLE

✛

Wasn't 'til mid-afternoon Isaac got close enough
to shout to his beast, and it wasn't 'til an hour later the
thing let him any closer.

"Hey, lightning!" he'd shout.

At first he was angry with the creature. But once his
anger wore off and he could see it was no help he started
to coo the name.
"Lightning."
"Heey lightning."
"Hey, you; lightnin-in-a-bottle, git yer ass back
here!"

"Ya got all my stuff son!"

He followed the horse all the way down the hill.
He followed it east, about a mile on toward
Waitsburg before the thing finally settled enough to take
on water in the Touchet river. And he knew it was his
chance and, pissed though he was, he couldn't be mad

toward the creature really; though he certainly wasn't happy.

"Hey, boy," he whispered as he came up close, and as the horse drank somemore.

"member me? I'm the one owns all that stuff strapped-to ya."

"Sure'd be nice if I could have it returned."

And the horse did let him nearer, to a couple feet away, then lifted its head and just looked at him; but to where its muscles were tense and it was shivering all over and its eyes were wide still and it's ears were shifting, between its owner and back up on the hill, and behind it, and across the water, then back again; to where Isaac couldn't hold much against it. It was young still and never had come across a cougar before. So Isaac found a stump nearby and he just sat and looked upon Lightning, which he'd just finally found his name for.

They were supposed to finish that day and be on their way back south by now. And before, maybe, the kid, knowing a man was on his hill and coming after him, mighta turned hide afterall. But now, with this cougar business, he kinda doubted it. Not since Isaac now owed his life to the boy, and his climbing a tree with only one arm, and his marksmanship which, despite that one arm, was pretty good indeed. So instead he had a feeling the kid, in the sweetness of his youth, would likely become confused by this event into thinking now that the hunter might spare him.

But the boy would learn soon enough, about duty, and necessity, and survival.

But for now Isaac just imagined Constance up on his hill this very minute with a smile upon his face thinking how he just turned the tables.

And then he imagined tomorrow and watching that smile come *off* that face as the boy come to realize that saving a bountyman's life don't change a thing. Cause the law's the law and a job's a job.

But either way Isaac took a breath and then looked at this steed of his and he held out his hand. And this seemed to settle Lightning a bit 'cause the horse, after a moment, came on over and mouthed at his hand, and then Isaac had him.

THE CONFRONTATION WITH CONSTANCE LOWREY

✚

Next morn, up on the homestead, all was quiet.

And the rocks still stood atop Mr. Piedmont's entombment.

And the same grey horse, likely once-belonged-to the deceased, still occupied its same pen beyond the half-built house.

But there was another horse; a brown one, walking loose upon the property, which was recognizable immediate as belonging to Constance; so that Isaac, settled low in the grass, knew that at last he had his bounty.

And soon-enough Constance himself emerged from the shelter, looked round, then got some water from the pump.

And the huntsman waited, and after-a-while he saw smoke rising from inside the building and knew

99

Constance had made a morning fire, and this the
huntsman took as his cue and stood, slow, rifle-in-his-
hand, and started his way toward the building.

And around the corner he half-expected to find
Constance gun-in-hand, but instead what he got was the
boy just crouched down low in front of his fire, holding
a pan over it and cooking up an egg. And when the boy
looked up he didn't seem surprised.

"Constance Lowrey?" the hunter asked.

"Yes," the boy answered, but stayed squat-down
beside the fire.

"That Mister Piedmont? Out uner those rocks?"

"Yes."

"You shoot'im?"

"No."

"Who did?"

"I don't know. Just found him out here, shot."

"You say ya jist *found*'im?"

And Constance did not answer this immediate.

"You xpect me ta buy that?"

"Look mister. I don't know who you--"

"I'm a bondsman's hunter, an you are my bounty."

And this threw Constance off and it was clear,
immediate to the hunter, that Constance was no criminal
and had not the slightest of the criminal's experiences,
and in fact was just a boy caught-up in something he did
not understand. And for just that moment the hunter felt
sure Constance was telling the truth.

But he'd learnt long ago never, ever, to think on

such things. Not for one moment. Because such was not his place. He was not, nor would he be, paid to pass judgement on the reality of an accusation. His job was *only* to bring in an accused to face justice.

Nothing more.

Never.

But still he could see all over the boy's face; this kid was smart, enough to know he was under suspicion, but he did not have the slightest notion that such a thing as a bounty even *could* be placed upon his head.

"Look mister," the boy finally stammered, "I don't... care who you are. I'd like you off my property."

"Son," Isaac retorted, "I'm sure you can put two an two together so it cain't be too much a surprise you been charged with the murder a Hector Piedmont. So you an I're gonna ride down ta Walla Walla an yer gonna turn yerself over ta the law."

Constance rubbed his neck, with his one good arm, but did not move nor even stand but just stayed squatted there and watched his egg cook over the fire.

"Sir, I'm sorry," he boy finally spake, slow, "but I'm not goin, with ya; because I didn't, commit, a murder."

And Constance just set there and tried to maintain his calm; but anyone with a half-good ear or one workin eye coulda told the boy was scared near-to-death.

"Beside," the boy carried on, "don't you need somethin more'n just showin up on my property to put a gun on me?"

And Isaac caught himself with a smile.

"So this *is* your property."

"Close enough sir, an I think that means you need ta get off it!"

But the hunter just cleared his throat;

"The domain a the enforcement agent," he began,
"that's me—*is a continuance of an original order fer
imprisonment. Whenever they may choose ta do so,
they may seize a principal*—that's you—*an deliver'im
up to'is discharge; an if it cannot be sodone at once
they may imprison'im until it can-be so-done. The
enforcement of-such may be exercised in parson or
by agent.* Agin, that's me. *The agent may pursue'im,
inta another state; may arrest'im on the Sabbath, an if
necessary may break-n-enter'is house fer that purpose.
Such seizure is NOT made by virtue a due process.
None is needed. Instead it is likened unto the arrest, by
SHERIFF, of an excaped prisoner."*

"What's that?" the boy finally asked.

"Taintor vee Tay·lor, U.S. Supreme Court, eighteen
seventy two. That's my warrant son. That's the rulin
gives me authority ta enter upon your property, seize you
up, an take ya with me; whether yer dead, in this case, er
alive."

And Constance, by now quivering visible, did not
have a thing to say except to keep an eye on his egg.

But as the huntsman watched, the boy gave no signs
of thought toward flight and his eyes weren't searching
for a nearby object nor a route to abscond neither. Rather
the boy was still caught-up in seeking to defend himself.

"Mister," the boy repeated, "somethin here…
don't… set right. Sir. And, I'm just not… keen, to go
with ya."

But the hunter wasn't moved, and his rifle was still

pointed to the boy's face, and in fact the huntsman's
finger was settled against the rifle trigger; but as the
boy was in the middle of cooking and wasn't giving
indication he was even thinking of running Isaac decided
to entertain the lad, just, maybe, 'til he finished his egg.

"You wanna explain yourself," he asked the boy.

Constance flipped his egg, with just his one hand no-
less and no spatula, with just a flick of his one wrist.

"Yes, sir, I do."

And then the boy looked up and made very clear his
intention, to reach out for his plate, which was nearby on
the ground. And the hunter nodded and allowed him his
plate and the boy grabbed it and set it nearby the fire.

And his fork too.

Which he set on his plate.

"So," Constance began, "I'm down the hill a-ways,
felling tree down the ravine; far enough away ta hear
a rifle? But maybe not a revolver, ta give ya some
impression. Anyhow I hear a blast, which isn't so
uncommon cept... I just hear'd the one shot."

"Kay."

"So what's funny bout that is, Hector never gets
game in one shot. But really, as I get ta thinkin, what's
very strange's that, I thought, the rifle's back on the
homestead. In fact I know its back on the homestead
cause somehow it's my fault he forgot it," and Constance
rolled his eyes. And then he flipped his egg to his plate,
set the frying pan down and scattered some dirt to quell
the fire.

"So," the boy continued, "my first thought's
maybe it's Nancy, Piedmont, ol' Hector's wife, took
the trek and brought it over to us. Or maybe there's an
emergency nearby, or for all I know someone's come

round with another spat gainst Hector; and there *are* a few a those.”

“So I’ve gathered.”

“Well I wish I’d listened but I’s in the middle of a log at that time and I guess I kinda figured if it’s an emergency I’d hear more, which I never did, so I just finished up with my allotment and turn back up the ravine oh maybe round an hour fore dark.”

“Kay.”

Constance took a moment to chop up his egg, and to eat it.

“Course when I come back,” he continued, “Hector’s dead. Shot in the damn face—pardon me.”

“But,” the boy added, after a moment of silence, “there’s no gun in sight, so he didn’t do the deed’imself. An then there’s all this dust, all kicked up everywhere, all over’im, only what’s *real* odd bout it is the dust’s all caked up on *top* the blood, like the dust got kicked up *after* Hector’s shot awhile. So see mister, somethin’s goin on here.”

“Kay.”

“An *then* on top a that, where’s Bill; who’s been here stayin with us over the nights an helpin-out in the afternoon, but who ain’t nowhere to be found since it happened? But on the day in question, by time I get back, the fire’d been set?!”

The hunter did not take the boy’s meaning as to how it’s pertinent the fire’d been set.

But after he’d waited, and after Constance did not continue, on account of finishing up his last bite of egg, the hunter asked.

"What's that mean?"

"Well you know Hector'd play every trick in the book ta keep from lightin a fire; on account a bein real bad at it. He looked like a donkey's ass tryin ta flint it goin. And the man *did-not* get the idea behind kindling. So… it's always I'd make the fire or Billy an *he* shows up mid-afternoons, after he'd get done breakin the new Stallion for those I·talians a couple ridges over. But when I get back an I find Hector's shot? Where's Bill? It's like he turn hide; only *I heard when the shot happened* so I know the general timeline an unless he got back earlier'n normal an then lit a fire for no good reason an then jist vanished mysterious *it don't add up.*

"And no, I *do-not* understand what it all means, but somethin about this stinks mister. Stinks like a polecat."

By now Constance was done his egg, and his fire was out, and the huntsman was out, of patience for all this yarn spinning; and Constance could tell.

"What'd you say your name was again mister? Isaac?"

"My name's the man holdin the gun ta yer face."

"Okay. Fair… I s'pose, given the circumstance. And I didn't mean ta give you the slip back there on the road mister. It's just… howda I say it?"

He looked at the bountyman a moment.

"I come ta suspect… the value a this land is, become higher than… the value a my life."

"How's that suppose'ta be?" Isaac asked, annoyed, then readjusted his grip on his rifle.

"Well you seen this property sir. This's four hunred acre. My parents come into it when the whole Rici clan perished, winter a seventy-two; but they couldn't keep it up. Not with what they have already. So originally it was ta be split three-way, tween us three boys and the three Piedmont girls was the arrangement. But Hector 'n Nancy lost Edith then Gladiola, which left just Narcissa for me. An four-hunred acre is a lot for a nineteen-year-old; but you don't start milkin midday…"

The huntsman just tightened the grip on his gun.

"Anyhow this was all in the seventies when the land up north here's jist dirt. But now, when we got wheat startin ta move, clear out ta Dayton, Hector's been talkin bout all these bankers knockin on'is door come every spring. 'These hills are turnin ta gold,' he'd say."

The boy then put his one hand up in the air, real slow, as anyone reasonable would with a gun on them, and then he stood.

"So yeah, when Hector turned up dead an Billy, who wouldn't know a horse from a beauty, turns up neither hide nor hair? Yeah, that puts me in a suspicious frame a mind."

But then Constance got quiet. But not the kind where some one's finished stating their peace; the kind where someone's about-to, state their *piece*, finally, after they've been working up-to it.

"You know," the boy finally squeaked out, "I ain't afraid ta say it. I cried, first day. Just left the body right there," and he motioned to the ground in front of the house where, now that he'd said it, the dirt was tossed up and it did look like there were some cakes of dried blood, "n just… cried."

"Hector ain't the easiest man to show tolerance sometimes, but he's… been my father-in-law, in essence, my whole life ya know? An we talked about this venture, an my marriage, an how life'd be, married to Narcissa, who if you gotta see'er you'd know don't sound half bad.

"We'd come out here on Sabbaths… all my life, an stake out here-or-there where we're gonna build…

"So yeah it took me a bit ta muster the … fortitude, justta make him his grave. An then I had ta put him in it, or under it or however…"

The boy drew a breath. And then his tone changed from sadness to anger:

"But then, once I came down from my sadness, my wheels started turnin; and it started to dawn on me, there ain't no reason for nobody ta *kill* Hector cept this deal we been workin on. And as I'm thinkin, this deal's in a delicate place for this period, tween now and the weddin, an that if it looks like I got heated, *and lord how everyone knows that was easy with that man*, ta where I lost my temper, well… this land's in a confusing spot.

"So after I took my day, to consider, it started to dawn on me too that I got just the week ta figure it out fore someone can move on it to my *dis*advantage."

"Kay."

"So first I go'd over to the I·talians, who nobody talks to cause it's just their son speaks a little English. But I get from him that Billy's skipped out on his deal there, which if you know Billy and you know a horse is irregular *to put it mildly*!

"So then I stop by *my* homestead an I ask around a little there, bout any strangers mighta come. I mean I even asked my two brothers if Ma an Pa been actin suspicious. But no leads there. So then I go inta town an I hear the Sheriff's due in but no one knows why. And then I come back for supplies an that's when I cross paths with you, askin bout a stranger to ya."

"Kay."

"Then," Constance continued, but at a measuredly pace, careful to control his temper and keep back any flashes might be misinterpreted—or interpreted—as anger, "That's when I know what's goin on. Somebody wants me off this land fer sure. Somebody's seen what it's worth, now we got the rail comin in, now we got wheat comin in, strong. Now the early folk already took the risk. Somebody's figured how easy it'd be ta get this acreage into wheat minus an owner!"

And for just a moment Constance wore a smug, righteous look upon his face, held his head up high, and back, and his eyes were bright and the ends of his mouth upturned. But it was just that moment and then he realized the hunter hadn't moved his gun, and that neither had the hunter changed the look upon his face. And then the boy's eyes lost their bright, and his mouth came down, and his chin came down, and then the teen in him started showing through; where triumph is not so easy as it would at-first appear; unlike defeat, which do come easy, and quick.

"So," the hunter finally asked, and blunt, "who?"

And he waited as Constance searched him and tried quick to devise some shrewd way to say he didn't know. But finally the boy gave in and shrugged and then just looked on our hunter:

"I have got, no idea."

"I was hoping," Constance did add, "Nancy would shed some light, but she says she ain't heard from no one since we set out over a week ago. So whatever scheme the party is up to, it's been in the works awhile."

And finally Isaac nodded, which, at first, consoled the boy.

Then Isaac spoke:

"Whelp," he said, "I'll give ya an hour, ta get yer things in order."

And the boy stared, flabbergasted.

"Sir, I ain't goin with ya!"

"Sorry ta break it to ya son," the huntsman said and aimed his rifle right to the boy's chest, "but ya are. So says three hunred dollars."

"Sir," the boy retorted, "if I need to post something let me talk with my parents."

"You may not be aware how our system works," Isaac said, "but I get my three-hunred-dollar from deliverin ya ta the County Court House. Think of it as what it is, more-r-less; a warrant out fer yer capture. *After* I deliver ya, *that*'s when ya work out the terms a yer release."

And this caused Constance pause and the hunter could tell from his eyes the boy's thoughts were running ten miles an hour!

"Walla Walla?" the boy asked.

"That's what I say'd," the hunter answered, "That's where we're headed."

And he waited just a little bit more for the kid to grasp the reality of the process.

But Constance wasn't looking to understand. He was thinking, quick, as the accused is custom to do, for a way out.

"Look, kid," Isaac said, "ya seem ta have yer head on straight. Think this through. You got yer story. Ya jist told it to me real clear. Ta me it's three-hunred-dollar ta make sure ya get ta the courthouse safe-n-sound. Then tell yer story ta the Judge an trust the Court ta handle it."

But Constance would have nothing of it.

"Or," the hunter continued, "otherwise, the letters on my flyer read dead just as well as they read alive."

And this was a bit much for Constance, and it was *now* his eyes started darting around looking for means to escape, and *now* that Isaac gripped his rifle tight and kept sure his finger was settled right on that trigger.

"I'm givin ya the hour as thanks fer takin that cougar."

But the boy started pacing, his one fist balled up.

"Sir," Constance pleaded, "let me ask you, do you *believe* my story?"

But the huntsman just smiled.

"Has nothin ta do with it."

"But do you *believe* it?"

The boy was desperate.

"Son, I get paid not ta care bout nothin cept what's printed on my flyer. I care bout my bounty an I do care bout my recovery ratin, so the more a pain in my ass ya git the more that dead part starts ta sound sensible."

"I ain't askin if you'll let me go!" Constance shouted, "I'm askin… what's your sense about it?"

"An son I keep tellin ya, my ears don't work that way."

But the boy was nearing the edge of what he could take. And the hunter was starting to plan where he might have to plant a bullet.

"Ya say, 'I didn't do it'," the huntsman said, "but all *I* hear is a bunch a squakin. I do not care son. I am not here ta care, bout no sad story nor no criminal conspiracy neither. I am here ta bring you in.

"That listenin back there, that's me doin ya the courtesy a lettin ya yammer, inpart cause ya mighta saved my life but jistasmuch cause it's easier ta lead a roped body walkin than drape a dead one over back my horse!"

"Look," the hunter kept on, "there's hunters see the word 'Dead' an quit readin. An they'd a shot ya fore ya even woke this morn, an that'd be yer justice right there!"

"Mister! Mister," the boy cut in. "I grasp it. I do. I mean… maybe, I'd like ta take my hour, an thanks, but to decide, maybe."

"Tween what?"

"Between goin in or, I guess, just… going now."

"Son, I don't *want* ta shootya--"

"And I don't wanna be shot. But what I'm askin, I guess, as a fellow citizen: Do ya think this's all just a bit suspicious? Ya don't even have ta believe me. Just, don't ya think it's all pretty strange? That I'd shot the father a my beloved? That I'da done that even when I been workin on this arrangement every day a my life up til now?"

Isaac sighed.

He did *not* lower his rifle.

But he did see the boy's aim. And he'd granted him the hour, and wasn't really particular on how it was used. And he *was* clear, as day, as to that line between interested citizen and executor of, or for, the law. So why not entertain the child, he figured, let him speak his piece and give him a shot to figure out himself how to answer to Justice for the suspicion he was under?

"So," Isaac finally said, "yer askin me ta play along."

"I would appreciate it."

"Shee·it," Isaac finally said. "I see. Fine. In that case? I *don't* know, if it's strange or not."

Of course Isaac did know. It *was* strange. But he'd learned by now never to entertain these desperate stories he was always fed by the accused.

But, again, as the boy'd shot that cougar when he may just as well've shot Isaac, and as his goal was, at the end of it, to get this boy to the county seat alive and wipe his hands clean of the whole affair, he decided he could suffer this hour, if it took even that long, to pretend.

"Part a me sees where yer comin from. Sure. Were that the real story, an--"

And here Constance raised objection, or tried to, to the huntsman's wording—the part about 'were it the real story'—but the huntsman already had his hand up and motioned to the boy to quiet down and listen, and if he were supposed to suffer the boy then perhaps the boy should suffer him; and all this was accomplished with nothing more than an experienced gesture of the huntsman's hand and an expression the huntsman had honed from years of shuttin' men up 'fore they even got started.

"Were that the real story," Isaac began again, "an *were* I ta find myself in yer boots; sure. I'd be suspicious. I'd even be real careful; a lot like, I s'pose, the way you're certainly bein careful now. Sure."

Then the huntsman took a deep breath.

"But since we're takin our time here, let me lend ya some education I picked up from doin this… oh, prolly close ta as long as you been alive.

"Ya cain't know son. No one can. No one can *know*. Even when the letter-a-the-law pretends it can, an pretends what yer gittin's justice, the lawman still knows the truth…"

And Isaac shook his head.

"…that *the* truth is only in the past kid. An ya cain't go back an git it. No one can, no matter how hard ya wanna piece it back together."

"But ya know what else? Like I say, *it don't matter.* Even what really *did* happen ain't where the law's concerned. What concerns the law is what'll happen in the *future*, an if it need-be prevented, how it is the law *can* prevent it. *That's* what our system-a-justice really is son. It ain't about yesterday's justice atall. It's about controllin what ya can a tomorra. So no I won't *really* believe ya, cause I learned by now there's really no way fer me ta know."

And this appeared to settle in with Constance. And the boy did consider it. And he was quiet a moment. And Isaac could tell from his eyes the boy was pondering and working out how this-all played into things.

"Thank… you, sir," the boy finally gave. "…but, how do I… convince, anyone, then, of my innocence? There's no proofs to help me out."

And the hunter sighed; not because Constance hadn't grasped what it was he was saying but because he knew that here there was a problem; the witness, and where the boy had not got one but the law did, in whomever Sheriff Dice'd talked to, which was likely this Bill character. And no matter how far Isaac would like to stay out of this business he did know, truth regardless, come Constance's word against just about any witness, the testimony of that witness would hold sway. So the bountyman tightened his grip on his gun and realized all-of-a-sudden that his face must've turned sour because Constance suddenly got to looking scared.

And then the hunter decided he'd had enough of this game.

"That's not my job," he said, real strong, so-as to shut the boy up.

But the boy retorted, "I think it is your job."

"An I don't give a shit."

"So you're telling me the law says you can kill someone on its behalf and then you're going to turn around and tell me it's not your job to decide if that killin's wrong or right? Ain't that decision what the law's trustin you to do?"

And Isaac turned his head and caught himself with something of a smile, in part because the boy was so right it stung.

"If I'd known we're gonna be philosophers this morn I'da made my coffee."

And Isaac took a breath. And he looked on the boy, who was so-suddenly facing matters of life and death, and who seemed to be getting quite agitated, and squirmy you could almost call it. And he thought on how here just in this past week the boy was setting out to start a fresh life and now he'd been cheated out of it. And the hunter took another breath and let it out real forceful, and then he started talking again:

"You want me ta tell ya the court'll deliver ya

justice, in the form a yer freedom, cause otherwise you'd rather jist take a bullet here an now?"

The boy took a moment, but he did nod.

"An I *want* ta tell ya the court'll set ya free an exonerate you a guilt, just so you'll shut up an start walkin!

"But the truth is, that jist ain't a promise I can make."

"Then how can you expect me ta go with ya?"

Isaac waved the barrel of his rifle in the direction of Hector's grave, "How do *I* know you didn't kill that man?"

Constance thought on this.

"Fair. That's… fair… But I didn't."

"That ain't the question boy. The question is, how do I *know*? I'm just a man collects bounty. I ain't the investigator. I ain't a Sheriff. I ain't hardly yer Lawyer. I don't even work this territory specially. I ain't equipped, in other words, ta make those kinda speculations. That's what the Court's for."

And Isaac felt pretty good about what he'd just said, like he'd really let the kid have it and laid down some solid facts, and like the only thing the kid could say to follow it was, 'yessir, you're right. Let's get goin.'

But instead Constance just looked at him kinda funny, to where the hunter put his finger right back against that trigger so he could get a shot off in no time.

"I'm, sorry," Constance finally whispered, "sir…

"I really gotta go."

"Go?"

"I'm sorry mister. Like, I gotta … shit. I gotta go."

And that finally made sense. The boy looked in that way, and it made sense him getting squirmy.

"It's gonna hafta be where I can see ya."

Constance looked around.

"What if I go behind a tree?"

"Howda I know you didn't stash a gun in that tree?"

Constance shrugged.

"Well… *you* could pick the tree," the boy offered, then added, "I'm sorry sir. I really am. I just, really *haffta*. No games."

But Isaac just stood there looking on Constance, his gun still held up, and considered whether to let the boy mess his pants, just to take a harsher tone—and to get this damned show on the road—or whether to let the boy do his business; since this' the one-arm had saved his life.

"You ever have this happen before?" the boy asked.

"Jist bout eery time I bring in a live one."

And the hunter watched the boy's eyes for those tiny signs a man's lying. But all he saw was, well, a boy, who needed to shit.

"Fine," Isaac finally said.

"Where? …can I do it?"

The hunter pointed out side the house.

"Jist squat out in the field."

"Okay," the boy finally did say, and then put his one hand up in the air again and made his way out of the half-finished house and out toward the field.

And the hunter followed close behind, his gun on the boy throughout.

And he watched the boy's eyes, close from the side, for even the slightest sign. And he was ready to pull the trigger and fell the boy at the slightest hint. And he'd never feel bad about it. Not so long as the kid gave him probable cause.

But the boy did not.

"That's good," the hunter finally decided, and Constance stopped and with a quick one-handed effort dropped his drawers.

And rather than look for some chance at flight the boy just searched the ground for a place to stand, and for some grass to use as wipe.

Now it was not the hunter's policy to give his prisoners privacy, though he did not personally enjoy seeing their private parts, the way he thought a few of the others might. But he did make it a point to inspect such regions, for weapons for one, but also for the insight it offered him as to how these men thought on themselves, and treated themselves, and maintained themselves.

And here on quick examination he found that Constance *did* care for himself and washed thorough, enough so he did not carry the red rash common to the criminal.

But then he already knew this boy was a farmer.

Still, as the boy did his business Isaac found, strange enough, he did have to respect this kid. And as the boy struggled, with his one hand, to balance and then, when he was through, to clean himself, Isaac did note the boy's approach. Constance was not one to pity himself. Nor did he seem to be one to give up, nor even allow himself frustration. And in this the hunter marveled on the boy; that even under a gun, and wiping his rear with just his one hand, the boy managed to carry dignity. This, the hunter determined, no matter what ultimately came of the kid, he would not forget.

Of course this was hardly the first time he'd found something to admire in one under his charge, and he was plenty aware that these desperate, resourceful people are often the ones to give the least warning when they see opportunity to flee, so he did not lift his gun off the boy, nor did he lighten his finger on the trigger. But regardless he did allow himself to admire the things admirable in the boy the same.

"So I guess," Constance finally spoke, as he pulled-up his drawers, and as he struggled with his buttons and then his buckle, "what it all boils down to is just… do you, trust, the law?"

"I do," the hunter said, "without reservation."

"With all due respect, even at my age I seen enough of its shortcomings," the boy came back.

And this did anger Isaac.

"The law," the hunter retorted, "is what makes thisall work kid.

"People already tried goin it without, so long ago we're startin already ta ferget, but that's been done. Trouble is, without law there's no consequence, ta nothin. An that's jist anarchy."

And the hunter took a breath, but kept on talking.

"I mean hell, *this* land here usedta be lawless. An I worked out in it. Usedta be everywhere. Was the law a the fist or the tomahawk or the arrow or whathaveyou. Then soon-nuff was the law a the gun, an now ain't that kinda what yer complainin bout right here? Yer Hector's dead an yer tellin me you don't want *no* justice?"

"I wasn't--"

"So ain't parta that submitin yer *own* self ta such justice?"

"That's not what I'm saying."

"The hell it ain't," the huntsman near-shouted. "We whipped this land inta shape, kid, while you was still sucklin on yer mama's teet!" And the huntsman shook his head, "An it's out here still, in these very hills, right here, tryin ta hide—eery which way—from the seats a order. I mean *everyone* who makes it has a law. Everywhere. Even in your far-off, exotic local·ity. They're all different in de·tail but they all have law the same. Cause… cause civilization—civility itself—jist don't work without it."

And here the huntsman had to pause, for breath; but he couldn't even stop long cause the boy had him so worked up.

"I mean look at the Indian!"

But Constance was quick to interject, "You know sir I met the Chief of the Walla Walla. Run into'im on the road with my Pa, on a trip down to the City. Not at all what ya hear. And you know what he said? He said they's just after peace. Same as anybody else."

"An look how well *that* worked for'em."

"But sir that's a double-edge sword. Cause as I heard it the law's hurt the in'gin smuch as it's helped'im. And that seems very much germane. Cause right now

I'm weighin out whether-r-not *I* can trust the law. And that's what I'm askin you, honest, whether or which way I'm goin with ya. I seen, already in just my few years, men stripped a what ought ta be theirs by the wrongful application a law. And now you show'n up, you're tellin me you're here ta dispense, justice, as if it's fairness? or like it's just plain right. And that's just not what I seen."

"I'n't say it's right. I say'd I got a job ta do, an I'm doin it."

"But you *are* saying the law is right."

"I'm sayin the law makes things right."

"But do you trust it? Or… I mean, do you trust the men operating it?"

"Do I trust the law men?"

"That's what I'm asking."

"Boy, who do you think yer askin it to?"

"Well, you said yourself some bounty men'll just shoot you, won't even give a man half a chance. You trust them?"

"That's jist bounty killers."

"I guess I'm unsure on the distinction."

"Well, we're men, charged *by* justice."

"To do a job?" Contance filled in, "But you're not law men?"

"We're their dispatch. The bounty man is an *agent* a justice."

"But, *do you trust'em*?"

"Ya keep askin me that son, like the answer's gonna change."

"Well, cause I know the answer you're sayin. But I also know the answer's… in the head … of any *reasonable* man, like yourself, who, as you say, *don't* just shoot a man before giving him a chance. Why do you do that sir? Why, if the money's the same, don't you just take aim at anyone wanted dead? I have to imagine it's cause you *do* believe in the law. And I do too. I see what it's worth, and I know most the time the law's just words on a piece of paper. But that's just the trouble sir. There's shortcomings. And this here situation is one-of them."

The bountyman sighed.

He *was* moved by this boy. But that was distinct from his job, and it always would be.

"Son," Isaac finally said, "I think you're confusin my gratitude toward the incident with the cat for my usual process. Normally I do not suffer *no one* like this, cause usually they ain't fortunate-nuff to've saved my life. But do not let it go gittin yer head outta proportion. Yer goin in whether you feel the law's at yer service r not. An trust, whether yers r mine, at the enda the day, ain't got nothin ta do with it. Yer gittin down ta that County seat an like it or not the man put in judgement over ya will be the one ta decide yer fate."

"And you're fine with that?"

"What's not ta be fine with?"

"I DID NOT KILL HECTOR!" the boy shouted, his eyes watered up. "And whoever… set this up to look like I did; he clearly set things up for you to come round to see I was removed. And you don't strike me as accomplice to that plot. But if you take me in sir, you are."

"So."

"So?"

"What plot, boy? Yer land, yer arrangement, yer future? That don't involve me. Not cause it's good or cause it's bad; kid, I got nothin ta do with it sides what I been hired for. But the cause-an-effect of it? Ain't on me. I'm jist a contractor."

"So it does not bother you to think you might be a part of something isn't right? Something … something… *criminal*?"

The bountyman sighed.

"Let me tell ya bout somethin criminal kid. Lets talk'bout Hector, an how he's dead. Let's talk'bout people all up an down this territory fall prey ta the most vicious, most vile, most destitute men ya ever-did meet! That's what *I* been doin this past lifetime son. I been stoppin *those* men. I been *huntin* those men, an bringin *those* men down, an makin'em face ta *their* crimes, boy. That's *my* job. That's who *I* hunt, an who *I* consider, an who *I* deal with.

"This here? This's side work sfar as I'm concerned. An yer little drama, compared ta those, ain't much. Ain't much ta the family seen their mother an daughter raped fore their eyes. Ain't much ta the parents come-cross their kids tortured an cut up an all sortsa other things ain't at-all pleasant ta talk bout.

"But here *you* are, whinin 'well I don't know… if it ain't fair maybe I'd rather jist die n haffta deal with it. Maybe if I cain't get *my* way that's the law's fault, cause it ain't good'nuff at dispensin me *my* justice, I want.'"

"Sir!" the boy countered, "Ain't a complete argument. I ain't sayin it ain't hard, an I ain't sayin you should know bout me. I already concede, I'm goin with you. I just gotta question what kinda criminality is goin on here. I mean look at me sir. Can't you see I ain't a criminal?"

But Isaac laughed.

"Son, thingbout the worst of'em… you never would tell. They's so sharp, so cold, you learn real quick this post ain't bout knowin nuthin. This post's bout one thing: like I keep sayin, sbout bringin yer bounty in. An that is it."

"But can't you see the weakness in it?"

"No. I don't see how ya figure."

"Look at me. You can't make *any* judgement? On how I suffered loss enough, in seein my whole... life's plan shot out from under me? Am I not lookin right?"

"Like I say'd, I don't get paid ta look at ya. Not that way."

"And you don't look at them neither? You can't tell *any* difference?"

And the boy just stared at Isaac.

And Isaac stared right back.

And it wasn't long before that stare grew uncomfortable.

"Sounds like they pay you not to look at *anyone*."

"Ya know," the hunter finally said, and raised his gun up, because he'd let it droop, "you make yerself too much a pain in my ass I'll cut yer hour short. An ain't ya got nothin ta do ta set the property right fore ya leave?"

Constance took a breath and did think on that a moment.

"Yessir. I'm sorry. Just… my life is on the line man."

"Ya get used to it."
And then Constance shrugged and then started looking around.

"I suppose I better turn Sugargrass loose, if I won't be here ta bring her water."
And the two started to walk that way.
And the hunter, who was still worked up, more than he'd thought, kept on.
"Ya think yer the first ta find'is life hangin in the balance?"

"It's the first… to have… *my* life…"

"Alright son," the huntsman conceded when he heard Constance's voice clamp up, "I'll give ya that."

"Marty here," the boy squeaked out, and motioned toward the horse standing free in the distance, "I always let roam, so *he'll* stick around an get water as he needs. But Sugargrass always runs."

"Hector couldn't train a horse neither."
And then they reached the gate to the pen and Constance opened it but did not shoo the horse nor give her any attention but just unlatched the gate so-as to make sure that when Sugargrass got restless she'd find her way out.
And then, with a long gaze cast toward his own brown horse, Constance took the hint and began a slow march back over toward the half-built house.

"Any problem if I leave a note?" the boy asked.

"No," the hunter replied, "you may."

And Constance got to looking around and grabbed a tool or two that had been left outside the shelter.

And as he did he turned to his captor.

"I don't suppose you got any paper?"

"No."

"Pencil?"

"No."

Constance looked around.

"I don't suppose you'd let me use a chisel?"

"Fraid not. But once we get south the Court'll send dispatch."

And at this Constance drew a slow breath, and then he nodded.

He picked up a few more tools and things, slow and careful, and moved them under the cover.

"So, sir," the boy finally spoke, while he organized some more, "say you're the judge in this matte--"

"I'm not, but okay."

"Right. Well… I'm just workin through thisall in my head again and first off I keep thinkin, I ain't got no alibi. None that'll hold up anyhow. I was off by myself cuttin lumber. An no we ain't had no gun up here ta do the shootin, but then I mighta just done myself in by heading back out to the farm where Hector's rifle's stashed."

But the hunter just kept back, and kept gun on Constance.

"For that matter," the boy continued, "just on the

devil's advice, what's ta say I didn't stash a gun up at my folk's place? or just out in the hills somewhere?"

"Good question."

"Yeah. Isn't it. For that matter anybody in fifty miles knowsa Hector's temper, and everyone's jist gonna think, well, the man had it coming, and ain't it just too bad he got under the boy's skin. And mister, that just wasn't how it was tween Hector an me. I never even imagined it."

The boy sighed.

"But I've got no proof of that."

And by now Constance was mostly done, it seemed. He just leaned against the wall and looked at the hunter and rubbed his neck.

"So the only thing I… just kinda am wondering … is, to a man such as … what's my chance a walkin?"

"There's just the one way ta find out."

And at this Constance shook his head.

"Sir, you are an open an shut case."

But the hunter did not make effort to respond. He just watched the boy and he kept counting down this hour he'd promised.

"But sir, you know where I'm coming from. I don't know exactly what the punishment for murder is, were I to be so accused--"

"Convicted," the hunter corrected.

"Okay. Right. But think what that's gonna do. That kinda mark don't rub off, sir, even when it's put on the wrong man."

But the hunter just shrugged.

"That's life kid."

"Doesn't sound like justice."

"Maybe not in the short view."

But the hunter was watching Constance real close now, while he still had about half his hour left but things were getting pretty well buttoned up and Constance, he could see, was finally starting to come into confrontation with this lot he'd been cast.

"Trouble is," the boy threw out, getting smarmy, "this whole doin just makes no sense."

"Already say'd that."

"Yeah, well I was about ta say bout the only way it does make sense is in light of you're here to bring me in at the behest, whether you know it or not, of whoever conceived of this deception."

"Okay kid."

"In other words, someone's using the law to their own *unfair* advantage."

"Kay."

"So, seeing how that seems to be the case, then when I throw myself down, the justice I can expect won't be any kind of justice at all will it?"

And the hunter sighed, even though he knew the boy could very-well be right.

"So I mean, what am I really looking at here mister?"

The boy's eyes were wide.

"Seems to me what you're offering is a one-way trip to either the hangman's noose or so many years behind bars it amounts to the same. I'm walking into a trap!"

And the boy waited.

And the hunter, Isaac, just stared, cold.

He'd been here plenty of times, and he knew where

this always headed.

"So are you really going to play a part in this?"

And then Isaac had enough.

"Look, kid. It's time. Don't put this on me. I ain't got a choice in the matter. I don't bring ya in an what? It's my ass on the line."

"Not your life."

"Yes, it is. Like I already stated, how do I know you're tellin the truth? How do *I* know you're walkin inta a trap? I let you go an I'm an accessory to a murder. Kid, I ain't puttin my neck on the line for no sad story. *End of it*. I'm sorry son."

But the boy pleaded: "This can not be justice!"

"Son, this is the rule a law." And Isaac tightened his grip on his rifle some more.

"Now," the hunter continued, "you need anything else done or should we get this show on the--" but Constance bolted, and before the hunter could even think twice he'd pulled the trigger and there was a blast and a fine mist of blood and the boy was, all of a sudden, on his back on the ground.

He'd got the boy through the right side of his chest.

This was not what the hunter had intended. If he'd had opportunity to take aim he'd've shot the boy thought the left side, through his heart, so it'd be only a matter of moments before the boy bled out and was gone. But through the other side, he'd just punctured Constance's lung and maybe blew apart a couple ribs, and it'd be hours, if not days, before the boy would succumb, left untreated.

So now the hunter had a choice.

He walked up, stood over the boy, who was now
writhing around and coughing blood and gasping on
account of having now half the lungs to go with half the
arms, and the boy looked up at Isaac and his eyes were
the widest they'd been.

This boy was not prepared for death, even though
he thought he was, and now he was scared, and in all
likelihood, though not in total certainty, he was about to
die.

Isaac had been absolutely in the right to shoot. There
was no question. And while the law's preference was
to prosecute a living man it had no problem passing
the record's judgement on a deadman the same. So
the hunter's chief incentive was to get the body down
south first and get it down living second. But it was his
subsequent interest which troubled him; those matters in
which his mandate *did* leave the dispensing of justice to
him. Because in this case it turned out he did agree with
the boy. This happening *was* suspicious and the law *was*
subject to abuse, and it was the money, not conviction,
prescribed the whats and hows of the performances of
his duties. And this did mean that when it came to his
handling of Constance, and his shooting of Constance,
he was *not* acting to his personal preference at-all but as
an agent of someone else's; that of the Sheriff over the
land.
Yet as he stood over the boy, and as he watched
blood pump from the boy's chest, he knew his post did
leave him in charge of what should be done next.

On the one hand he might save the boy, if he rode hard and dispatched south direct, but it would be hard on the boy and in some likelihood the boy's mind may wind up damaged, or he may be left alive in body only.

On the other, as he looked down at the kid, he saw that the boy was, though aged just into manhood, very much a boy still, in that he'd not-yet had time nor near-experience to fully appreciate death, in all its looming veneration; so that now it was clear in the boy's face that even despite the pain of a punctured lung, and even at the prospect of noose or bars, Constance simply did not-yet want to die.

But still, everything inside Isaac told him that the humane course was to finish the job, and to do it quick.

"Well…" Isaac's voice trembled.

"Wha'da we do now?"

But the boy just writhed, and gasped, and was want, somehow, the pain should stop.

"I am sorry," the hunter finally said, "I am. Not the way I preferred it, either or. But now this's where we find ourselves."

Constance looked up, and it wasn't anger he saw in the boy's eyes but pleading. Not cowardice, but if the boy weren't so young you might call it that. Simply put, though he did want for the pain to stop, Constance was not-yet ready to swallow his bitter pill.

But Isaac was.

And with regret, he pointed his rifle down on the boy.

And Isaac pulled the trigger.

And Constance was gone.

THE PROPERTY,
NOT ITS OWNER

✝

Though it did not affect him so much at that time, in the ensuing years the incident up on Piedmont's plot came to leave the huntsman disenfranchised with his profession. And though he did not regularly dwell upon the goings-on of the matter, regarding the Piedmonts and the Lowreys and the fate of the pro·per·ty so involved, he did view the plot as a touchstone of a kind; in those darkest moments most-oft between sleep and waking, when a man questions the grand things and the complex becomes, if for just those few moments, clear; as to whether or not his life had been on its right track.

And at some point he decided that his life no longer was and that enough was enough and very suddenly he took up the profession of selling insurance one day with the event of Constance's death some ten years behind him.

And he did sell insurance for another ten years still, and did well at it for all the stories he had on the tragedies could befall a man, which he'd seen with his own eyes, and on-which he was so-positioned as to offer

unique and frightening insights with which to scare his
prospects into signing upon the doted line.

And he did see it as a spreading of civility, perhaps
which satisfied because it was a brand of civility he was
unable to spread as a bountyman.

And soon he was nearing his retirement and as he'd
insured enough by-now to begin to enjoy the leisures
of life, and had-not a family upon which to bestow, or
serve, his riches, he took again to travel, which he'd
always enjoyed, to 'cast his net farther for the company'
and to explore new-and-untapped markets and to see
who's where when it came to the insurers, and to report
all this back to his company for the record; to leave
behind at least some legacy.

And it was in this work that he found himself
traveling up the great Gorge of the Columbia, out of
his home base of Vancouver now, in Washington, the
State now, with his eye set on the Snake river and far-off
Lewiston and Clarkston beyond.

But upon this trip, coming past the split in the
mighty Columbia where the Snake branched off, he
heard mention of the name of the nearby town of
Prescott in passing as a fellow passenger gave the name
in discussion, and heard also, by chance, that the railroad
did leave nearby Wallula for Walla Walla and that it
then-ran through Prescott on its way out to Dayton; and
that this included regular passenger service. And he
decided right then to put-off his regular work awhile,
which was on his own schedule beside, and to take the
trip.

And the train ride was pleasant.

He'd before spent some time in-and-around Walla Walla and here-and-there the scenery outside was still familiar and began to revive in him all sorts of memories; of tracking this villain or that, shooting this man here and felling that man nearby there.

And when he arrived in Walla Walla that eve he settled into the Genevay Hotel, nearby the station; which was a modern place with electric lights in the lobby and gas lamps in the rooms, and even steam for heat. And he arranged for his accoutrements to remain and the next morn he caught the early train to Dayton.

But the rail to Prescott was *not* familiar, even though he'd been on that road a time or two when it was still the Mullan trail.

And the town of Prescott itself was now unfamiliar, as there were now several local streets across the Dayton road and whole neighborhoods, and Spalding Street was now-called Division street and the Grange had relocated out of the town, and there was now a schoolhouse and even the once-grand Prescott Hotel was run-down and had lost its signage and looked empty.

But it was his reminiscences of the Pleasant Pheasant which most aggravated his disappointment as, though the place was a café still, it was now called Melvina's, and in not-nearly-so-fine a font.

He passed through the town, though, on foot, even in his business attire, and headed down the road for Dayton.

And soon the walk became familiar again afterall.

And the hours passed, and as he walked the road, for the first time in many years he recalled his old horse, ol' Lightning, and how that animal had gained its name here on these bluffs, back when the beast wasn't old atall.

And he recalled how the horse, like Old Iron before, *had* learned the huntsman's ways and *had* become a skilled companion before finally meeting his own old end from colic.

And soon Isaac's stomach ached, and his back ached, and his legs, and he knew at last the damage ten years out from any real work had done him. He felt nothing like the man who'd last traveled this road twenty years the younger.

But at last he came to the Pepper creek and he looked up that slope and considered that this could be close enough.

But, as he looked around, and as he considered the ache that had come to consume the whole of his old body, he thought he'd come all this way already. What good would it do to stop now? So he set foot before foot and soon he made his way up, and by afternoon he stood atop the bluff and looked out once-again at that view, upon the Blue Mountains that stood before him still, unaltered.

And then, after his look around, he identified the plat where once-had-sat a half-built house. And he found the trees which had once-framed its view, and under which Mr. Piedmont has once-been buried. And he knew from these the spot where the poor young Constance had died.

But all that was gone now and over with; and not just gone but tilled under, as the land was now in the full golden splendor of wheat; acre upon acre of it, near as far as the eye could see.

But without homestead.

And he scanned the horizon and gazed in the view, and in so-doing he happened to catch the form of a man atop a horse in the far-off distance, seemed to also-be surveying the field.

And the man had spotted him. So, not want of any suspicion, Isaac walked over, toward the man. And the man did the same:

"HALLO!" Isaac finally shouted.

"Hallo," the man shouted back, "how do you do?"

"OH, FINE," Isaac shouted, "JUST FINE."

"Anything I can do ya for?" the man asked, and from here Isaac could see the man was a farmhand, about twenty years younger than himself.

"No. Nothin particular. I had some business up here once upon a time."

"That right?"

"It is, bout twenty years ago."

"Huh."

"Just always wondered what become a the place."

"Belongs ta Brainerd Dice at present. Not sure who had it when you's here last."

"Back then it was the Piedmont's."

"That right. I only been up here since ninety-eight myself. I'm from California originally. But Mr. Dice had it at that time. Course he was Sheriff Dice back then."

"Sheriff Dice," the old huntsman finally repeated, and once-again he could see that man's grey must-ache and the flow of his hair and he could once-again smell the smoke of his tobacco.

"He still around?"

"Lives in Walla Walla."

"Oh, he's back *there* now?"

"Never left."

"Oh?"

And Isaac thought that strange. But regardless, that was the end of it so far as he and this farmhand were concerned.

"Well," he said to the man, "I thank you. Got ta be back in town fore tonight's train, so I better be off."

"Alright. Good luck to ya."

"I do thank you sir. You have a fine evening."

"Will do. And, sir? You want me ta pass anything on to the property owner for ya?"

Isaac thought on this.

"No. I do thank you though. The matter concerned the property, not its owner."

MELVINA'S

✛

Melvina's was still a dowdy little café, and still cheap, but it did not strike Isaac as nearly so charming. The wallpaper, which was the first thing that found his eye, was of a soft lavender pattern that ran up the walls in barely-there stripes that made Isaac think they shouldn't've bothered. But regardless he was greeted warmly-enough by another young woman and he was given choice to sit wherever, so he took his old seat, far from the windows in another two-chair in the corner.

And he looked over the press-printed menu waiting for him on the table and saw they now stocked items regular and they'd now an ice-box. Then he noticed they'd got their electric lights and gas to their stove.

"Can I gitcha somethin ta drank?" the young girl asked.

"A coffee'd be fine."

"Okay, sir. Coffee. Looked over the menu yet?"

"Not yet."

"Okay. I'll git yer coffee."

"I thank you."

And the girl went over to the pot and poured from-it

coffee already on the boil and brought it to him.

"Here ya go. Jist holla when ya ready."

"Well, I was curious if I might get your recommendation."

"Well," the girl drawled, "that depends on what yer in the mood fer. We git reg'lars in here all the time order on they mood: They's in a hungry mood we git'em a steak out the cooler. They in a tired mood we cook'em some pasta. They--"

"Pasta?"

"Yeah?"

"Here, in Prescott?"

"We got some I·talians up the road aways."

"Oh, sure."

"You know'em?"

"Uh, never met, but I heard tell."

"Well she's a real good cook. Makes us pasta fresh. Useta farm up northa here. She cans up our sauce too."

"Sounds a charm."

"So you want the pasta then?"

"I think so. Thank you."

"Sure thang sir."

And the girl went over to the kitchen and started on boiling some water.

And Isaac watched, for he was no longer so wrapped up in things as he was when he was younger. In fact as he'd aged he found he'd begun to *enjoy* observation, even more than contemplation.

And he sipped his coffee, which was awful.

"Say, miss?" he finally asked.

"Yessir?" she replied.

"Ya know, I *have* frequented this place a time or two, but it's been awhile."

"That right."

"Back then it was called the Pleasant Pheasant."

"Oh yeah?"

"Ever heard of it?"

The girl turned to him.

"No-sir."

"Oh," Isaac sighed.

"Well…" he finally said, "I suppose that's the way it goes."

THE OLD KIRKMAN PLACE, ON COLVILLE

✛

The ride back to Walla Walla was quiet, as Isaac was near-the-only passenger on the train. And that night he stayed again at the Genevay Hotel. And the next morn he wandered down Walla Walla's Main Street and took some breakfast at The Red Apple where he read a copy of the *Walla Walla Bulletin*—which'd just started in print earlier that year and was already the third largest paper in the region, as he read above the paper's head line. And in it he caught a piece about a newly formed Symphony in the town and was taken quite by surprise to find among its benefactors a *B. Dice*:

"Scuse me, mister?" Isaac called to the young man standing behind the counter who had been staring blankly out the window and polishing glasses and stacking them away.

"Yessir."

He was a gangly fellow, loose at the limb, but seemed friendly enough.

"You happen ta know where I might find an old man by the name a Dice?"

"Dice?"

"That's it."

"I'm afraid I don't sir. The name doesn't sound familiar."

But another guest, down the counter, spoke up. "Old *Sheriff* Dice? Is that who you're lookin fer?"

"Yessir it is," Isaac called back.

"He's down the road just a ways, on Colville, up near the station, in the old Kirkman place."

"Oh," Isaac said, "I been there. You say *he's* in the Kirkman place?"

"Yessir. William died, if you were not aware, more'n ten years ago now."

"I wasn't."

"Yeah, so his kids went off ta school; an so the old Sheriff kinda tookover the place."

"That so."

"It is."

"Well," Isaac said, and began to fold up his paper, "I thank you much."

"Don't mention it."

FIRST PIANO CONCER·TO, SECOND MOVEMENT

The walk up Colville street was short and quiet, as this was may-be ten in the morn and in general the townsfolk were settled in to their work for the day already.

Getting into summer it was warm, too, and the sky was about as clear a sky as they come.

And it wasn't long at-all before Isaac came to the Mansion, which he'd been aware of for some time as the sometimes-residence of the wealthy Kirkman family, who were from England but who'd spent a good part of their time here in the Valley.

Mr. William Kirkman had made for himself quite a mark on the local scene, once upon a time, back when the huntsman had been around. The man had been, as Isaac recalled, involved in the formation of the local State Penitentiary for one, into which many a bountyman'd seen their bounties go to rot; and many of whom, he reckoned, might still be inside. So it did sadden him a little to think Mr. Kirkman was already passed, but more it piqued his interest that the Sheriff should come to occupy his place; for the Kirkmans' Mansion was, at one time, the finest residence north of San Fran and, it seemed, maybe too ostentatious a residence, even in retirement, for a humble man-of-the-law.

And now, here, standing out-front, the place remained, though in slight disrepair, still a very fine residence and very much befit more a businessman than a public servant.

But regardless Isaac was here and might just as well take the few steps there, he thought, to the front door, and make his re-acquaintance.

And when he reached the door he rapped upon it, and waited, and after some time a woman answered, in her middle age and quite sweaty.

"Hallo?"

"Hello ma'am. I am wondering if I might find the old Sheriff Dice here?"

She eyed him skeptically.

"Mister don't take solicitations."

And without even thinking, because he was so-used to going door-to-door in his solicitations of insurance, he said, "That's only secondary to my business here ma'am. Would you tell'im we've met before, up north, in the town a Prescott? I believe the name a my bounty was Lowrey. Thought he might wanna sit an reminisce a minute, since I'm in town."

She did not answer but just shut the door.

But Isaac knew a sale by now. So he waited.

And sure enough, the woman opened the door just a few moments later:

"Mister remembers. An says it's good timin too. So come on in an make yo's way ta da left hea. He's in da back, gettin ready ta put on one a he's new music recordins."

"Much obliged ma'am."

"Uh huh." And the woman walked off down the hall.

"Hello?" Isaac called as he came around the corner.

He could see, past the sitting room, back near the piano, the old Sheriff set in a recliner beside an unusual contraption; looked like a large metal flower sprung up from a small polished wooden cabinet.

"Hey there!" the Sheriff bellowed. "Good timin ol boy. I was about ta put on a disk a music."

"That so?"

Isaac had heard-of such contraptions but had not-yet the opportunity to experience one.

"So," the old Sheriff mumbled, "Yer name a'gin?"

"Isaac, sir. I once run bounty for ya."

And the Sheriff looked him over awhile, and Isaac took occasion to do the same, and in so-doing he noticed the old man was not tremendously changed except he'd lost the button of hair, and his skin was wrinkled up some-more, but otherwise he still had that same mustache and even the same white gruff upon his face too.

And after a moment the Sheriff finally nodded his head.

"Yes. Yes. I member you. You brought in the Lowrey boy."

"I did sir."

Then the Sheriff shook his head.

"Tragedy."

"It was."

"Ya know," Isaac went on, "I heard your name in passin, an that you're still alive,"

"--ha! Surprised?"

"I was sir, a little, if I'm honest. An hearin it, an that you're so close, I thought I'd come pay you a visit."

"Well…" the old Sheriff said, "I'm glad ya did. Ya know what they say bout how misery loves the company."

And the two laughed at that.

"Say," the old Sheriff went on, "ever hear'd one of these music players?"

"Can't say I have."

"Well… you're in for a treat! This here's one a three plays disks in the whole Valley."

And the old man produced from behind his recliner a large paper-stock envelop and slid out from within it a large, shining-black platter upon which was imprinted a strange and curious texture.

"That right."

"Is. I just got this here come taday. Was jistbout ta put it on. Wanna hear?"

"Well sure," Isaac said, in genuine curiosity, "I'd be much obliged."

"Good," the Sheriff said, "here we go then."

And he leaned over and set the disk on the round plate made especially for it upon the cabinet. And he maneuvered an arm out over the disk so the fine point of the arm just touched the disk's surface. And this

produced a jarring jolt of noise from within the mouth of
the metal blossom which startled Isaac.

The old man then struggled some, to stand first and
then to turn a crank sticking-out-from the lacquered
cab. And inside it somewhere a ratchet clacked and
then, when he was done, he adjusted his glasses to
see to check the label at the disk's center for some
small instructions on which adjustment to make to the
contraption.

"Jist need ta dial the speed in."

And Isaac himself leaned forward and looked over at
that label.

It read *DISQUE POUR GRAM-O-PHONE* but the
rest was too small to read from his distance.

And soon the contraption begun to spin the disk
anyhow, and then from inside the blossom a tone
funneled out.

It was the sound of a hundred fiddles; some being
worked with a bow and some being plucked; which
soon-formed into a slow, broody tune.

And then a piano begun to play.

And the old Sheriff leaned back in his recliner.

And Isaac leaned against the piano, in the room
there, and just stood, and just listened.

At first the softness of the piano struck him as
melancholic.

But there was a force in the song too, hidden beneath
the sorrow of those soft notes, so the music carried some

power he felt familiar with, like a song of nature herself, captured, somehow, by nothing more than a piano and a symphony of fiddles, and then locked, somehow again, inside this strange black disk.

It was like a song where nature carries out her will against you; but to where you can't hardly hold it against her.

For her will is her own, and what man could ever stop it.

And then the piano struck on a happier tune.

It was a tune that became quick and fleeting, like a sky full of spring-time sparrows, flitting hither and yon.

And then the tone changed again and the piano left off and the strings started back up.

"You like it?" the old Sheriff asked.

"I do," Isaac said. "What is it?"

"S french music. Someone named Camille," he checked back to the envelope, "Saint Sanes. I believe he's a feller though."

And the music changed again, to a slower, brooding *pluck*, and then a note, and then a *pluck*, then a note again; and this went on for some time.

Until the piano returned once more.

"This's'is," the Sheriff checked back to the envelop, "first piano concer·to, second movement."

"Ah," Isaac said.

And then the piano took on a deep tone and
made a powerful tune that settled down in Isaac's gut
somewhere and grabbed him up unexpected and, he did
believe, moved him.

And that such sounds were coming from a
mechanical device amazed him too and added greatly
to the effect, so that even though the sounds from the
contraption were but a faint echo of the volume he'd
heard in the music of a full band, the setting, here-being
so unexpectedly in the glorious old Kirkman's mansion,
listening to such powerful music, and mechanical music
at that, was near-overwhelming.

"You heard," the Sheriff asked, over the music,
"bout the new symphony they got together here in
town?"
"As a matter-a-fact I did."
"Well, I been thinkin bout havin'em play this piece
in the full orchestra."
"That right."
"I am a patron, an I do think it would be powerful."
And Isaac nodded.
"It would."
And he listened some more.

And then Isaac turned to the man and, as the music
was quiet in this part, and pretty, the former hunter
spake:
"You know, I never did hear what happened with
that business up on The Piedmont's Plot."
"Oh…" the Sheriff gave, "it was a *tragedy*. An
absolute tragedy. The land set in trust fer… years, while

the lawyers mulled it over."

"That right."

"Tis."

And here, and it could have been his imagination, but Isaac did imagine that the music took on a sinister tone; with the piano side-stepping down, lower and lower; octave after ornate octave.

"Infact it's I who finally stepped in an opted ta buy the property outright, just ta settle the matter."

And now the strings faded so it was just that piano, settled low, down into dark music.

The kind of music that stirs a man's soul.

"That was mighty big a ya."

And the Sheriff thought on this a moment and then grabbed for his pocket all-of-a-sudden, then looked up at Isaac and smiled, embarrassed he'd grabbed for something wasn't there.

"Ya know," the old man then muttered, "it was the ladies—those Piedmont ladies—who lost the most. I mean they'd lost near-everything. Poor Nancy'd lost her husband an Narcissa lost'er groom.

"Those were dark times."

"I imagine they were."

"I ended up buyin her out too," the Sheriff confessed, though maybe he didn't know it was confessing. "Land wasn't worth much but I saw to-it she's taken care of. Nuff ta put Narcissa ta school back-East."

And the Sheriff shook his head, then added, "Hard times…"

"They were," Isaac repeated. Then he turned to

his old Sheriff, "Land looks like its up an runnin now though."

"Well I should say. What with the railroad come through. Put the two remainin Lowrey boys ta work on it s the funny thing."

"That right."

"Yep. Managed it for quite a few years fore they both finally run off n got married."

"Yeah, I hear'd you were over *all* that land out there. An I was a little surprised just cause as I recall you weren't too fond a the northern country."

And the Sheriff nodded and tugged at his must-ache.

"No," he finally said with a long look and a bit of a twinkle in his eye. Then he leaned back in his recliner.

"But, ya know, for us lawmen—an I wonder if you feel the same—but for us lawmen, there's only one thing, really, I think is worth havin in this world, almost more n anything."

"What's that?" the huntsman finally asked.

"It's peace. Mister.

"Peace."

And the old man took a breath. And though he knew it was his imagination, Isaac felt he could once-again see smoke pour from the old Sheriff's lips, as he looked his hunter dead in the eye, and as he exhaled.

"An as I recall sayin," the old Sheriff finally gave, "so far as that place go, I only ever heard but a couple complaints."

THE END